Patricia's Secret

By RUTH DAGGETT LEINHAUSER

Illustrated by Evelyn Copelman

SCHOLASTIC BOOK SERVICES

NEW YORK • TORONTO • LONDON • AUCKLAND • SYDNEY • TOKYO

© 1956 by Ruth Daggett Leinhauser. This edition is
published by Scholastic Book Services, a division of
Scholastic Magazines, Inc., by arrangement with Holt,
Rinehart & Winston, Inc.

21 20 19 18 17 16 15 14 13 12 11 10   6 7 8 9/7 01/8
Printed in the U.S.A.

CONTENTS

MEETING FATHER

PATRICIA LOWELL knelt on the broad seat below the south windows of her bedroom and gazed with aching intensity down the driveway that encircled the house. At any minute now, she knew, a car would come through the stone gateway at the end of the drive and approach the house.

In that car would be her father.

A little shiver ran through her, and she thought, I believe I'm quaking. I've always wondered how people quaked. Now I know.

A car slithered into the graveled drive. Patricia sprang to her feet and then stood still, her icy-cold hands pressed against her burning cheeks. She closed her eyes tightly because she didn't want to see her father get out of the car and come up the steps. It was terrible—it was perfectly terrible to have a father coming whom she hadn't seen for almost seven years, not since she was three years old.

5

For all of those seven years, ever since her mother had died, Patricia had lived with Aunt Mary and Aunt Sue, her great-aunts. She couldn't remember her father at all, for she had not seen him during that time. He was a major in the Air Force. Patricia knew that he had been in service all during World War II, and since then he had remained in the service and had been stationed in strange places all over the world.

Aunt Mary and Aunt Sue had talked to Patricia a great deal about her father—she must never forget him, they said. They had told her that he was splendid and kind and handsome and all the things a father should be, but they were also enthusiastic about the Lowell cousins who lived in Albany. Patricia thought that the cousins were simply impossible, so perhaps, she reasoned, her father was impossible, too, and her aunts didn't realize that he was because he was a relative.

I wish he hadn't come, Patricia thought furiously now. I don't need him! I don't need him at all!

There were footsteps in the hall and then a gentle tap at her bedroom door.

"Come in," said Patricia, amazed to hear her voice emerging like a little squeak.

Aunt Mary opened the door and stood there all excited and fluttery.

"Darling, your father is here. After all this time, he's really here. Let me see how you look—oh, too sweet for words in that rose linen dress! Your hair—yes, Aunt Sue did your braids beautifully today. My, your father is going to be surprised to see what a little lady you've grown up to be. I'm sure he thinks that you are still just a baby."

All the way down the stairs Aunt Mary talked and talked. Patricia didn't say a word. She clung to Aunt Mary's hand so tightly that her own fingers ached. Her feet grew heavier and heavier, and her stomach felt as though a tennis ball were bouncing in it. By the time they reached the door of the living room her head was whirling. At the door Aunt Mary withdrew her hand from Patricia's, and said breathlessly:

"Go on in, dear. I—I have to slip out to the kitchen for a moment to see about dinner."

"Is Aunt Sue in there with him?" Patricia whispered desperately.

"No," Aunt Mary whispered back, "I believe she's in the kitchen, too."

"Why do you both have to see about dinner?" came Patricia's anguished whisper. "Where's Cora? Isn't she getting dinner?"

"We don't. She is. I mean Cora is getting dinner," whispered Aunt Mary. "Your Aunt Sue and I think it would be nice for you to see your father alone first.

Aunt Mary disappeared. It seemed to Patricia that she just evaporated.

At the front end of the hall, the big door stood wide open. For a moment Patricia played with the idea of darting outdoors and away, then her common sense asserted itself. She squared her straight shoulders, raised her chin a little, and marched into the room in which her father waited.

In the big room the rays from the late afternoon sun slanted in through the Venetian blinds onto the highly toned old mahogany furniture so dearly familiar to Patricia, onto the multicolored bindings of the books in the low shelves, onto the prism candlesticks and the Dresden figurines that adorned the old-fashioned mantelpiece over the fireplace. It was a beautiful room, but it seemed just then to Patricia's apprehensive eyes a vast, ominous cavern. Out of its depths came a tall figure. A friendly voice said casually, "Hi, Pat."

Pat, indeed! Aunt Mary and Aunt Sue had never permitted Patricia's name to be shortened. Pat is not a dignified name for a little lady, they would insist gently.

Patricia could find no words with which to answer that salutation, but after a second her head cleared, and she could see. The stranger didn't rush to her and pick her up in his arms as she had been afraid he might do. He just stood and grinned at her, his dark eyes twinkling as though he and she were sharing a joke, his teeth flashing white in his deeply tanned face. Patricia's eyes started their inspection at his feet, swept over his splendid uniform, over the wings above his heart, on up at last to his face.

He said, smiling, "I'm just as much afraid of you as you are of me, you know. As a matter of fact, after I rang the doorbell, I almost lost my nerve about coming in. If Aunt Mary hadn't come to the door just when she did, I think I would have bolted for the car and driven off."

I wish you had, Patricia thought bitterly. The aunts were right about your being handsome, but just the same I wish you hadn't come—I don't need you—

Into her silence her father said, "Shall we sit down?"

He was treating her just as though she were grown up, not sitting down himself until she was seated. Patricia sat down on one of the big chairs with dignity and held herself very straight and folded her hands in her lap. Her father sat down in a chair facing hers, and his eyes were still twinkling.

"I suppose you've been pretty happy here?" he asked thoughtfully.

Patricia's heart turned squarely over. Just from the

way he asked that question she KNEW. He didn't say, "You ARE pretty happy here." He said, "You HAVE BEEN pretty happy here."

He had come to take her away.

Panic swept over her. Why didn't I think of that? she asked herself wildly. Do Aunt Mary and Aunt Sue know?

She sat up even straighter and laced her fingers tightly together. She said fiercely, "I'm happy every minute. I'm the happiest person in the whole wide world."

"Well, that's fine," her father said, blinking a little at her intensity.

Just then Aunt Mary and Aunt Sue came fluttering in, both of them very pink and excited. Patricia slid off her chair and went to stand by Aunt Sue, who was the bigger and the stronger of the two. Aunt Sue put an arm around her and squeezed her and said that dinner was ready, and isn't it wonderful, Patricia darling, that your father is here. Then they all went into the dining room.

The big table was set with the very best damask cloth and the superbest gold-band china that the aunts wouldn't even trust Cora, who had worked for them many years, to wash and put away. There were pink roses from the garden in a low silver bowl in the center of all this splendor. Cora was admittedly the best cook in Middleport, and tonight she had outdone herself. Never had chicken been more beautifully browned. Never had mashed potatoes been fluffier. Never had hot biscuits been flakier, but Patricia couldn't eat a thing, because the tennis ball was bouncing around in her stomach again.

Her father had come to take her away.

She couldn't look at him, and she didn't want to

listen to him talk, but she couldn't help listening because he told such interesting things. He had been in China and in Japan and in India and in many European countries, flying everywhere, meeting fascinating people, having amusing adventures. Patricia had never heard Aunt Mary and Aunt Sue laugh as much as they were laughing tonight. She looked at them wonderingly. How could they laugh? Didn't they know, didn't they even suspect, that her father was going to take her away?

Presently they stopped laughing when Major Lowell's voice grew serious while he talked about his own plans. He had been recalled to the United States, he said, to instruct young fliers on a big air base in California; he could stay in Middleport only tonight and tomorrow. The day after tomorrow he must start for his new base.

The tennis ball in Patricia's stomach quieted down a bit. She thought happily that she couldn't possibly be ready to go away off to California in such a short time as that.

Or could she?

Aunt Mary and Aunt Sue could frequently accomplish the seemingly impossible when they put their minds to it.

The tennis ball began bouncing again.

After what seemed an endlessly long time dinner was finally over.

"May I go to bed now, please?" Patricia asked Aunt Sue softly as they were leaving the dining room.

Aunt Sue's hand flew to Patricia's forehead.

"Darling, do you have a temperature? Don't you feel well? I saw that you weren't eating—"

"I feel just fine, Aunt Sue. I'm sure I don't have a temperature. I—I'm just tired or something."

10

"It's been a strain waiting to see you, since we got your cable saying that you were coming," Aunt Mary said apologetically to Major Lowell. The major's brown eyes laughed at Patricia as though to remind her that he and she shared a joke.

"I'm sure it has been," he said quietly. "I think I'll want to go to bed early myself. Good night, Pat."

"Good night," Patricia said in a small voice and flew up the stairs.

In her own room she closed the door and locked it behind her. Then she flung herself across the bed, heedless of the best pink bedspread, and gave way to the tears that she had been holding back ever since she had heard that her father was coming. She hadn't known that she could cry as hard as she was now without making any crying noises. She got so interested in crying without noise that pretty soon the tears stopped coming and she sat up, feeling a little ashamed.

After all, she thought, father's not really a dreadful person; he's better-looking than any other father I've ever seen, and he certainly talks more interestingly than any other father I've ever known—in fact, he talks like a book.

Patricia sat on the edge of her bed and listened to the gentle rumble of voices coming from the veranda directly underneath her own windows. Her father and the aunts were sitting out there in the evening coolness. She wondered what her father was telling about now, and half wished that she hadn't been in such a hurry to come upstairs.

Perhaps he wasn't telling about the strange places he had seen. Perhaps he was telling Aunt Mary and Aunt Sue that he was going to take Patricia back to California with him.

Surely the aunts wouldn't let her go! Patricia knew

11

how devotedly they loved her, but wouldn't they have to let her go if her father wanted to take her? She supposed gloomily that she really belonged to her father, even though the aunts had almost always taken care of her.

She walked across the room and sat down on the bench before the little pink ruffled dressing table that Aunt Mary had given her for Christmas last year. She turned on the pink-shaded lamps that had been one of Aunt Sue's Christmas presents to her, and stared at her tear-swollen face in the mirror. She couldn't go away from here to live somewhere else, she thought bleakly—she just couldn't. She couldn't leave her own room and her own house. She had to go to school, to her own school. She had to go to Sunday school, to her own Sunday school. She had to take piano lessons from her own piano teacher.

Her father was going to an air base. Little girls didn't live on air bases. Or did they? They shouldn't anyhow, Patricia thought fiercely. An air base was probably like an army camp. A few weeks ago she had seen an army camp when a company of soldiers of the National Guard had come to Middleport in big army trucks and had camped for a night in the park at the edge of town. Practically everyone in town had gone out to see the encampment. Cora had taken Patricia.

Patricia thought of the little pup tents she had seen in which the men were to sleep. Why, those tents were so little that she couldn't even stand up in one of them. How could she possibly live in one?

The little girl in the mirror with the wide gray eyes and thick golden braids was Patricia Lowell. Patricia Lowell couldn't go off to live on an air base. She lived in a big stone house that was always warm

12

in the winter and cool in the summer. She lived with Aunt Mary and Aunt Sue and Cora, who all helped her with her arithmetic and her practicing and cooked all the things that she liked to eat and took care of her when she had a cold. She lived in Middleport, Iowa, where she knew every man, woman, dog, cat, and canary bird by name.

The grandfather's clock on the stairway landing struck nine, a half hour past her bedtime.

Patricia got up from the bench and undressed slowly. She turned off the lights and got into bed. As she pulled the fresh, cool sheet up over her, she remembered that she had not washed her face and hands or brushed her teeth, and she didn't care.

"If I have to go away from here and live on an old air base, I'll never brush my teeth!" she sobbed into her pillow. Then because she knew that was silly she had to stop crying to smile a little, and before the tears would come again, she was asleep.

The blow fell the next evening.

Outside, it was raining, a gentle, warm June rain that filled the air with a hundred flower fragrances. Patricia and the aunts and Major Lowell sat, after dinner, in the library. Aunt Mary and Aunt Sue were knitting afghans; their fingers flew so fast that their needles clicked rhythmically. Patricia was knitting a yellow anklet to match her yellow sweater. Her needles didn't go fast enough to click; in fact they moved so slowly that she thought she probably would outgrow the sweater before she even finished one anklet, much less two.

Major Lowell sat in a big chair where the light from a table lamp shone upon his face and his crisp, dark hair.

On the surface everything seemed serene and peaceful, but Patricia was deeply uneasy. All that day she had avoided her father whenever possible, thinking foolishly that if he didn't see much of her, he might forget about taking her to California with him, if indeed he were planning to do so. She had been tense and on edge all day, relaxing only a little when old friends of her father came to see him, or when he was away from the house making short calls himself. This evening, as she sat struggling with the confusing four needles and the yellow yarn, she thought:

He can't be thinking about taking me with him; if he were, he would have said something about it before now. He's going to leave tomorrow morning. I almost know that he can't be going to take me with him, but, oh, I wish that I could be sure he isn't!

As the thoughts churned in her mind, she became aware of the fact that no one in the room had spoken for quite a few minutes. She glanced up in quick fright and found her father looking at her thoughtfully. He cleared his throat and said abruptly:

"Pat, when I learned that I was coming back to the States to be stationed here, I hoped that I could have a good long leave to give you and me time to get acquainted with each other, well enough acquainted so that perhaps you would want to go to California with me."

Patricia's hands suddenly turned so cold that she couldn't hold the knitting needles. She dropped them onto her lap and sat staring at her father.

"Of course," Major Lowell went on slowly, "we don't know each other at all yet, but I'm going to ask you to go with me, anyhow. We'd learn to know each

14

other on the long drive to California, and have quite a bit of fun doing it, I think."

For a moment it seemed to Patricia that she had lost the power of speech. She had to swallow hard before she could answer.

"Do I have to go?" she asked finally, her voice almost a whisper.

"Why, of course you don't have to," her father said, looking at her ruefully.

His words swept away Patricia's panic. She drew a long, deep breath of relief, and said politely, her voice quite natural again, "Well, then, thank you very much for inviting me, but I believe I'll stay here at home."

She saw the look of sharp disappointment that clouded her father's eyes, but she didn't care because he was disappointed. She leaned back in her chair, feeling breathless, as though she had been running hard to escape from something dreadful.

Aunt Sue had put down her knitting, too, and now she spoke decisively.

"Patricia, my dear, it isn't quite as simple as that. Your Aunt Mary and I have been talking it over since your father told us last night what was in his mind. We know that every little girl needs a father, and you need yours even more than most do, because you have no mother. Your father needs you, too. Your Aunt Mary and I feel that you must go."

Dazed by this unexpected attack, Patricia turned her eyes to her Aunt Mary. There were tears on Aunt Mary's finely wrinkled old cheeks, but she nodded her head firmly.

"Your Aunt Sue is right, darling. You must go with your father."

They were all looking at her anxiously, unhappily.

15

Patricia looked from one to the other of them in horror. She cried desperately:

"But tomorrow! How can I possibly get ready to go tomorrow?"

Her Aunt Sue said briskly, "Your clothes are always in order. It will take only a little while tonight to pack a traveling bag with the things you will need during the trip. We'll send the rest of your things in a trunk by express."

"No!" Patricia cried, springing to her feet. "No, I—"

"Let's forget that I ever mentioned it," Major Lowell said sadly, but Aunt Sue spoke firmly.

"Trent, no ten-year-old girl is wise enough to decide a thing like this. It's too bad that Patricia hasn't had time to get used to the idea, but that can't be helped. Of course she is going with you, and when she gets over her first feeling of strangeness and homesickness, she will be very happy, I know. Come, Patricia, we'll go up now to pack your bag, and then you must go to bed, because your father wants to get an early start in the morning."

Always, during the seven years that she had lived with her Aunt Mary and Aunt Sue, Patricia had been able to wheedle them into almost anything, but now, after looking into Aunt Mary's kind old eyes and then into Aunt Sue's, she knew that this time they would remain unmoved by any amount of tears and pleading. She stood up very straight, and said on a deep breath:

"All right, then, I'll go."

To herself she cried furiously, I'll go, but I'll be back soon—I'll be so naughty that he won't want me to stay with him—he'll be glad—glad—glad to send me home!

PATRICIA'S RESOLVE

PATRICIA didn't know then, or ever, how the idea of being naughty had happened to pop into her head. She had never been a mischievous little girl. She had heard one or the other of the aunts say innumerable times to their friends:

"Yes, it would be hard for us, as old as we are, to have a child to bring up, except for the fact that Patricia is such a good little girl. She's always reasonable and always thoughtful and obedient. It's a pleasure to have her because she is so sweet and good."

All through the restless, wakeful hours of the night, her last in Middleport, Patricia's resolve to be naughty strengthened. Being disagreeable and unpleasant would be easy, she thought—it was only being good that was sometimes hard. The more she thought about the idea the better she liked it. No one would want to keep a very bad child, she told herself.

So delighted was she with her plan and so confident

of its success, that she didn't feel tragically sad when she kissed the aunts and Cora good-by the next morning, and settled herself in the big shining new car that her father had bought as soon as he had landed in the States. They all looked so grief-stricken that Patricia longed to tell them not to feel bad, that she would be back soon, perhaps in a week. Well, no, probably in about two weeks. The trip would take several days, and once in California she might want to stay for a little while to see it—that is, if she could possibly stand living in one of those tiny tents for any time at all.

She was actually going to California. She was actually traveling.

As the car left Middleport and gathered speed on the highway that led westward, Patricia's eyes were bright with excitement. She had always wanted to travel, and she had never been anywhere at all, except occasionally to other small towns near Middleport, and once to the state capital, Des Moines. Until now she had counted that trip to Des Moines as the most exciting thing that had ever happened to her, but it was nothing compared with this. Why, now she was going to cross many states; she would see mountains and the ocean. She would see Hollywood. If the air base were not too completely impossible—

The air base! Patricia's heart dropped right down into her stomach at the thought of it. Aunt Mary and Aunt Sue had always been so careful of her; why, oh why, would they let her—no, MAKE her—go live on an air base?

"Pat, you're being an awfully good sport about this," her father said suddenly. "I know it's tough for you to leave Middleport, but the aunts were right, you know, about us needing each other."

18

Patricia nodded, afraid that if she spoke, she would start to cry. There was something about her father's deep, tender voice just then that curled right around her heart. If he were someone else's father, she thought, I could like him quite a lot; I wouldn't even mind having him for my own father if only he were not taking me away from home.

"This is the second trip you and I have made together," Major Lowell went on pleasantly. "The first one was even longer than this one. I suppose the aunts have told you all about it—that you were born in Hong Kong while I was stationed there, that your mother died when you were not quite three years old, and that I brought you from China to Middleport. I don't suppose you remember anything at all about it, do you—about your mother or our house in Hong Kong?"

"Not really," Patricia said slowly. "I only sort of remember a few things, like running down a garden path to a gate and calling, 'Daddy, daddy!'"

"Yes, you used to run to meet me in the evenings when I came home. I would pick you up and swing you in the air. You were the cutest little curly-headed baby, always laughing. By the way, I haven't heard you say 'daddy' since I came back."

Patricia's cheeks began to burn. She couldn't—she just simply couldn't. The name daddy belonged to someone she had run to meet long ago, not to this stranger. To change the subject she said hastily:

"When I was just a little girl, I thought that I was Chinese, because I had been born in China. When I first went to school, we had to learn to speak a piece called 'I Am an American,' and I never would do it. One day the teacher noticed that I wasn't saying it with the other children, and she asked me why not, and I said, 'Because I'm not an American—I'm a China-man.' I never will forget how everyone laughed, even the teacher."

Major Lowell chuckled.

"We'll go back to China sometime, Pat. When I'm old enough to retire from the service, you and I will travel all over the world. Would you like that?"

Patricia remembered suddenly that she was already traveling too far from home for her peace of mind.

"Thank you, but I don't believe I'd care about it," she said. "You see, as soon as I grow up and get through college, I'm going to be an actress, so I don't suppose I'll have time to travel much."

She watched him from under her lashes to see how he was taking that. Whenever she said anything to her aunts about wanting to be an actress, they looked distressed. She had deliberately mentioned it to her father now, hoping naughtily that he would be concerned, too, but he wasn't. He asked her with interest:

"Are you going on the stage or in the movies?"

"I—I don't know," Patricia had to admit, because she really didn't know yet what she wanted to do when she grew up; she just liked to tease the aunts a little sometimes by telling them that she wanted to be an actress.

The day didn't work out at all as she had planned it. She had intended to ride along in suffering silence, sighing deeply now and then so that her father could clearly perceive that her heart was broken, but some-how she just couldn't seem to do it. All that morn-ing she found herself laughing at the things her father said, and talking to him as hard as she could. She had planned, too, to eat almost nothing on the trip so that he would worry about her, but when they stopped for lunch that noon, she was actually ashamed of her ravenous appetite. She ate and ate and ate.

The afternoon passed swiftly and pleasantly, too. Major Lowell was a careful driver and never took his eyes off the road, but he could talk as he drove. He talked so well that Patricia sat entranced, the strange countries about which he told becoming real and vivid to her.

"Where are we going to sleep tonight?" she asked, late in the afternoon when they were many, many miles from Middleport.

Her father named a city.

"We should be there about half-past five. That will give us time to bathe and rest before we have dinner. We'll have a good night's sleep, and be on the road again early in the morning. There's a good hotel there —I think you'll like it."

Patricia had never spent a night in a hotel, and she was perfectly delighted at the prospect of doing so. She loved the lobby of the hotel with the deep chairs all around it, and the big dining room with its excellent food, but best of all she loved her own room, number 520. It adjoined her father's room, with a shining white bathroom between, and she thought that she could live happily in it all the rest of her life. The furniture was maple; the draperies and carpet a soft shade of blue. There was a radio and a writing table. In the drawer of the table Patricia found writing paper and envelopes with pictures of the hotel on them, blotters, ink, pens, and even telegram blanks.

After dinner Patricia and her father walked around the downtown streets for a while, pausing often to look into store windows. When they returned to their rooms, Major Lowell said, looking at her doubtfully, "I suppose you know how to put yourself to bed?"

Patricia assured him that she not only knew how to put herself to bed but that she knew how to get herself up in the morning, too, and he told her a laughing good night.

When she was alone in her own room, Patricia breathed a long sigh of satisfaction. Never had she felt as grownup as she did now, preparing to sleep alone in her hotel room. She undressed and put on her pajamas and slippers, and then hung her dress and coat on hangers in the big closet. They seemed so little and strange hanging there all by themselves that she stood still for a moment, looking at them soberly. Then she went over to the writing table and examined the contents of the drawer again. She wished that she could send a telegram to someone; then she really would feel grownup. She thought of how Aunt Mary and Aunt Sue always fluttered and looked worried when they received a telegram. Thinking of them reminded her that she should write them a letter.

She sat down on the chair by the desk, dipped the pen in the ink, and wrote very, very carefully because she didn't want to make a blot on the writing paper.

Dear Aunt Mary and Aunt Sue:

Here we are in this hotel. I put an X on the window of my room in the picture. It is very nice here. We drove 350 miles today. I am well and hope you are, too.

Lots of love to both of you and Cora.

Patricia

She put the letter in her pocketbook to mail in the morning. It didn't seem possible, she thought, that it was only this morning she had left home. It seemed ages ago.

Suddenly Patricia didn't feel grownup at all. She felt very little and quite lost. I'm alone in a big city in a big hotel, she said to herself, solemnly. Of course, father is with me, but that doesn't count, because he is a stranger.

In a few more days she would be living on an air base.

An air base!

I won't stay there, she promised herself fiercely.

She went over to the desk and took out another sheet of paper. Across the top of it she printed in big letters: HOW TO BE BAD. Below that she wrote the figures from one to ten in a downward row. Then she sat frowning at the neat page. What could she do that would be bad enough to make her father send her home?

It was strange how hard it was to think of bad things to do. Finally she wrote after the figure 1— Don't practice.

Aunt Mary and Aunt Sue were very strict about practicing. Patricia felt quite pleased about item number one until she realized with a little sense of shock that of course she couldn't practice even if she wanted to—there wouldn't be any pianos or music teachers on an air base. If the aunts had thought of that I don't believe they would have let me come, she reflected. As a matter of fact, she felt pretty bad about it herself, for while she didn't like to practice, she really loved to play the piano.

She drew a line through item number one, crumpled the paper, and dropped it in the wastebasket.

I'm too sleepy tonight to think of any good badnesses, she decided. I'll just have to figure them out as they come along.

In the morning when her father knocked on her door, Patricia was already awake. She sprang up at once, and washed and dressed, and then began repacking her suitcase, wishing that she didn't have to leave the pretty room. When she took her brush and comb off the dressing table, she stood looking at them in wide-eyed dismay. Her hair! Whatever could she do about her hair? She had thick, curly hair that had never been cut. Every morning Aunt Sue brushed it and made two braids, one on each side of Patricia's head, which were drawn back to be braided in two fat pigtails.

I'll just have to do it myself, Patricia realized.

She pulled off the rubber bands that held the braids, unplaited the curls and began brushing vigorously. That part was easy and it felt good, but when it came to making the parts and braids it wasn't easy. Even by practically standing on her head before the mirror, she couldn't seem to make straight parts. The comb got tangled in a cluster of curls, and she had to yank so hard to get it out that tears sprang to her eyes. She had just finished making two very crooked side braids when her father knocked again.

"Almost ready for breakfast?" he called cheerfully.

"Do you suppose you could fix my hair?" called back Patricia dismally.

"Could I what?"

Major Lowell opened the door, came into the room, sized up the situation in one quick glance, and looked extremely doubtful.

"I'll do my best," he said.

His best was very bad. When he had finished, Patricia stood looking at herself in the mirror, and he stood looking over her shoulder.

"How often does it have to be done?" he inquired.

24

"Oh, every day—sometimes twice a day," moaned Patricia. "Whatever am I going to do? I look awful, just simply awful."

Then she drew a quick, deep breath, for all of a sudden she knew what her first naughtiness would be. Just as soon as she could get to a beauty shop, she would have her hair cut short. If there were no beauty parlors near the air base, she would find some scissors and cut it herself.

Often when Aunt Sue was giving her a particularly bad time with snarls, Patricia had begged to have her hair cut short. The girls at school frequently told her that it was a shame to have her curls plastered back into braids, and Patricia heartily agreed with them. Aunt Mary and Aunt Sue both admitted that they thought her hair would be nice cut short, but they always added:

"We just can't have it cut, dear. You know in almost every letter your father writes he asks if you still have braids. It would be a disappointment to him to find that they were gone when he comes home."

Here was a naughtiness made to order, but just thinking about it made Patricia feel guilty and unhappy and quivery inside. Being naughty isn't much fun, she thought, but I'm going to do it—I'm going to cut my hair! If father wants me to have braids, maybe he won't like me at all without them. Maybe he will send me home right away.

"Why don't you have those braids cut off?" Major Lowell asked, still looking at her in the mirror.

His words were such an echo of her thoughts that they made Patricia jump. She turned around to stare at her father in amazement.

"You—you don't want me to," she stammered.

25

"I think it's a fine idea," her father said, smiling at her.

"But in your letters you always asked if I still wore my hair in braids—that's why I had to do it, because you wanted me to—"

"Oh, not at all," her father said, looking surprised. "I just asked, because if you were changed in any way I wanted to know about it. I should like to see your hair all fluffy around your face."

Well, that naughtiness has certainly fizzled, Patricia thought dolefully. Then she looked in the mirror again at the straggling part in her hair and the very odd-looking braids, and said in a little voice, "I'd like to have it cut."

"Well, come along," her father said, smiling at her, "we'll have it done right after breakfast. There's a barbershop here in the hotel."

Patricia had never been in a barbershop before. While she was sitting in the shop with her father after breakfast, waiting her turn in one of the barber chairs, she looked the shop over with lively interest, and sniffed with appreciation all the fascinating hair-tonicky smells. It was a small shop with only three barbers. In one chair there reclined a man with his face swathed in steaming towels, which the barber kept replacing with even hotter towels. Patricia thought that the poor man must be suffering terribly. She watched him anxiously for a while, but he seemed to be enduring the ordeal very well, so she turned her attention to the occupant of the next chair. The man in that chair was being shaved. The barber ran a big, sharp razor over his face and neck with such flourishes that Patricia couldn't bear to watch.

"Do very many people get hurt in barbershops?" she whispered fearfully to her father.

"Nobody ever gets hurt," her father assured her.

In the third chair, there was a little, round old man with a pink face, and only a little fringe of white hair around the back of his bald head. He was having a haircut. He had so little hair that Patricia couldn't see why he wanted any of it cut off, but the barber kept snipping away.

At last the little round man stepped down from the chair, and it was time for Patricia to step up. She felt very strange when the barber wrapped her up in a big white thing like a sheet.

Maybe I'll look perfectly terrible without any braids, she thought, in sudden panic.

The scissors in the barber's hand hovered around her head, then clicked, and clicked again. In a moment or two her hair was lying softly against the top of her shoulders and fluffing out around her face. She stared at herself in the huge mirror with growing delight. She didn't look terrible—she looked much better than she ever had before. Her father's smiling nod of approval told her that he thought so, too.

During the rest of the trip, Patricia found that her short hair was a joy. It was easy to keep in order, and it curled beautifully. She loved to toss back her head and feel the curls brush softly against the back of her neck.

As a matter of fact the whole trip proved to be a joy. Her father was, she had to admit to herself, the best companion she had ever known. He made her laugh until her sides ached. He was interested in everything that she said, and he knew the answers to all the dozens of questions she asked about the country through which they were driving, and about the things they saw along the road. He taught her new songs, and they sang together as they drove along.

On the morning of the fifth day of the trip Major

27

Lowell said cheerfully, as they were starting out, "Well, this is the last lap of the trip. We'll be there tonight."

All the way across the continent Patricia had been trying not to think about being "there," but ever since she had awakened this morning, she had been thinking, tonight I'll be on an air base with all those horrible little tents.

"How big is it?" she asked in a shaky little voice.

"The Base? Oh, it's a big place."

"Will we—will we live in a tent together? Or will I be alone in one all by myself?"

Her father took a quick look at her face, and what he saw made him turn the car off the highway onto the side of the road and stop.

"Now what is this about tents?" he asked gently.

"Why, you know," Patricia faltered, "the tents we're going to live in at the air base. Aunt Sue says that anyone can get used to anything if he has to, but isn't it hard to get used to living in a little tent? Will we sleep on the ground or will we maybe have a big enough tent for cots? I hope it's cots, on account of bugs and things on the ground. And do the tents leak when there's rain?"

"Now listen," Major Lowell said firmly, as tears trembled on Patricia's lashes, "we're not going to camp out. We're going to live on one of the finest air bases in the world. We're going to live in one of a row of houses built especially for officers and their families, just about the prettiest little house you ever saw."

"In a house? Then we won't have to cook our meals over a campfire and eat a lot of beans and things out of cans?"

"Not a single campfire. Not a single bean," her father promised soberly.

Patricia leaned back in the seat of the car with a sigh of exquisite relief.

"I've been dreadfully worried," she confessed.

Her father turned the ignition key and started the motor. Then he looked at her and said slowly, "Look, Pat, after this when you're worried about something, why don't you tell me about it? I seem to have the impression that that is what fathers are for, to take care of worries."

In his voice was the note of tender understanding that made Patricia feel warm inside. I'm afraid that I'm going to have an awfully hard time being bad, she thought uneasily.

THE LADY OF THE HOUSE

IT WAS dusk when Patricia and Major Lowell reached the Base, but as they drove along its streets, her father called Patricia's attention to one thing after another. Patricia strained her eyes to see the great hangars, misty-shaped in the half-darkness. Street lights came on suddenly to aid her vision. She gazed with interest at the buildings her father pointed out to her, the recreation center, the indoor swimming pool, the fieldhouse, the barracks, and then a long row of houses.

At last Major Lowell stopped the car in front of one of the houses, and said, smiling, "Well, here's our tent, Pat. I wired Robert what time to expect us, and I see that he has turned on all the lights in the house to welcome us."

"Robert?"

"Haven't I told you about Robert? I should have, because he's a very important member of our family. He

30

was my Filipinio houseboy when I was stationed in Manila several years ago, and I've taken him with me wherever I've gone since then. He's our cook and housekeeper and gardener."

"A boy cook?"

"Well, Robert isn't exactly a boy. He's probably about forty years old. Here he comes out the door—he must have heard the car."

A beaming little brown man in a starched white coat came down the walk and greeted the major and the major's stupefied daughter with enthusiasm. Then he whisked the bags out of the car and led the way into the little house.

"You could almost put this whole place into the aunts' library," Major Lowell said, and Patricia, after some investigation of the house, decided that his statement hadn't been much of an exaggeration.

The house was built on a square, with the long living room making the front side, facing north; the dining room and a small sunroom were on the east; Patricia's bedroom and her father's were on the west; Robert's quarters and the kitchen formed the south side of the square. In the center of the square, with all the rooms opening onto it, was a patio, the first that Patricia, from Iowa, had ever seen.

Patricia was so tired the first night that the house seemed just a vague, pleasant blur to her, but she awoke the next morning to California sunshine, and with the desire to see everything in the house and on the Base.

Of course her room underwent her inspection first. It was done in fresh blue and white, with maple furnishings that were even prettier than those in the hotel room she had liked so much. It wasn't nearly so big as her room in Middleport, but it was a friendly little room, and it seemed to belong to her right away.

31

Just as Patricia finished dressing, she heard her father leave his room, and she ran out to join him.

"Good morning," Major Lowell said, smiling at her. "You look as though you had slept well."

"Oh, I did, and I've been looking at my room. I'm just simply crazy about it."

"Good. You must tell Mrs. Corrick so—it will please her to know that you like it."

"Mrs. Corrick?"

"Our next-door neighbor on the east. She and her husband, Captain Corrick, are good friends of mine. We've often been stationed in the same places. When I came here and found the Corricks living in the house right next to the one that had been assigned to us, I gave Madge the job of getting our quarters ready, so that I might start right out to Iowa for you. What do you see now that makes your eyes so big?"

"The piano," gasped Pat, "the lovely little piano."

"That's yours," her father told her. "Ever since you started taking lessons the aunts have written me about what a fine talent you have, so I thought you would want to go on with your lessons here."

"I do," Patricia said slowly. She turned away from the piano to look thoughtfully at her father.

"What's on your mind?" he inquired, his smile deepening.

"I was just thinking," Patricia said, with a queer sort of lump in her throat, "about how you got the piano for me and my room fixed for me—"

"I want you to be happy here," her father said.

They went into breakfast then, and while her father was looking over the morning paper, Patricia sat drinking her orange juice slowly and thinking harder than she had ever thought before in her life.

I'll have to stay for more than a few days, she

thought. Since Father has done so much to this house just for me, I probably should stay quite a while. Perhaps it wouldn't be too hard to stay all summer. I could go back just in time for school. And I think I won't start being naughty for a while. It wouldn't be fair to be bad right away on purpose, when Father wanted me to come so much and did all these things for me.

Suddenly she felt happier than she had since she had decided upon her campaign to make her father send her home, in spite of her sobering realization that a whole summer was quite a long time. But surely Father will think all summer is long enough, she thought; he surely won't be disappointed if I stay that long. I'll tell him in a few days that I want to go back for the opening of school.

After breakfast Major Lowell said regretfully that he had to report at once to headquarters.

"I wish I could take you all around the Base," he told Patricia, "but I'll be so busy the next few days that I'll have to leave you pretty much on your own. Ask Robert anything you want to know—he knows everything. And remember, you're the lady of the house now."

While he was talking, Patricia had walked with him to the front step. From the sidewalk he turned to call back to her, "Wander around and get acquainted with the neighbors if you want to. We're all sort of one big family here."

The lady of the house was lured by the bright sunshine to stay out of doors. For a time she sat on the step, her hands clasped about her knees, watching the activities of the Base, which had been quiet last night when she arrived, and was anything but quiet now. Several great planes, flying low, droned overhead. The strange-looking objects called jeeps scurried by on the street in front of the house. Two Air Force nurses, capes swinging from their shoulders, walked briskly by.

This is better than a movie, Patricia thought, pleased to find so many interesting things going on just beyond her doorstep.

She finally got up from the step because she remembered there were still a great many things to be explored. First she decided to follow the stepping-stones that led around the side of the house to the backyard. The backyard was small and disappointing. There was nothing there but the garage and a border of bright flowers and two trees, and the sound of Robert rattling dishes in the kitchen. The trees were very pretty, though, with remarkably shiny green leaves. Patricia had never seen trees like them before. She went a step nearer to them and then stopped short.

"Robert!" she shrieked.

Robert appeared on the kitchen doorstep, and Patricia gestured to him wildly.

"Robert, please come here quickly."

"Yes, Miss Pat. You get hurt?" Robert asked, hurrying out, dish towel in hand, his face screwed up in anxious wrinkles.

"Robert, there are oranges on those trees!"

Robert relaxed and began to fan himself with the dish towel.

"Very good oranges," he declared. "Four, six more days they ripe, and you pick some."

He went back into the kitchen, and Patricia, feeling a little foolish, walked around and around the orange trees, gazing at them in excited wonder. Of course she had always known that oranges grew on trees, but to know that they did was one thing and to see great big golden oranges actually doing it was quite another thing.

After a while she went into the kitchen. Robert had finished the dishes and was polishing silver.

"I like to do that," Pat said, so he gave her a soft cloth, and she sat on a high stool by the table and polished spoons vigorously. She liked Robert, and it was fun to listen to him talk, though sometimes he spoke such funny sentences that she had to think hard to figure out what he was saying.

"My father says you have been with him for a long time," she remarked.

"Major finest man there is," Robert said promptly. "Long years I work for him, and never mad does he get. Fine gentleman. Fine soldier. Maybe sometime he take you to fly."

"I don't want to fly," Pat said, shivering a little at the thought. "I hate airplanes, because they make so much noise and because they look so dangerous."

"Major best pilot ever has been. He come now to teach the young ones how to be good flier just like him."

The doorbell rang just then, and Patricia slid off her stool and ran to answer it, going across the patio to the front of the house, thinking how funny it was to have a little bit of a garden right in the center of your house.

There was a young woman on the doorstep, a slim young woman in blue slacks and a boyish white blouse, with short dark curls, and dancing brown eyes. With her was a dilapidated old pram that had once been a thing of splendor, and in it sat a very alert baby, clad only in a diaper. He, too, had short brown curls and dancing brown eyes.

"You're Pat, of course," said the young woman, smiling. "I'm Madge Corrick, and the baby is Spuds. He and I wanted to be the very first to welcome you to

35

the Base, so we dashed right over in our working clothes."

"Won't you come in?" asked Patricia, opening the screen door and feeling very much indeed like the lady of the house. It was the first time she had ever had a grownup caller all her very own.

"We'd love to. Just a sec, while I unstrap Spuds. How do you like his chariot, by the way?"

"It—it looks very comfortable," stammered Pat.

Mrs. Corrick laughed and plucked the baby out of the pram.

"It has a long history," she said, going into the living room with Pat and sitting down with the baby on her lap. "It was purchased in its original glory for Billy Carmichael. When he outgrew it, the Carmichaels gave it to the Duncans for their baby. The Duncans passed it along to the Simpsons for their Mary Anne. Now it's Spuds' turn for it. I'm afraid it's going to be in pretty bad shape for its next little owner."

She and Patricia laughed together.

"I think you have the cutest baby I ever saw. Do you call him—Spuds?" Patricia asked shyly.

"Yes, isn't it silly? There's no reason at all for it. His name is actually John Aldrich Corrick, Junior."

She gave Pat a swift smile.

"My dear, all of us who have known your father for so long could hardly wait for you to get here. We've seen so many pictures of you and heard so much about you that we feel as though we have known you from the time you were born. Your father was so excited when he left to go for you—you've no idea. We had fun getting the house ready for you. Do you like it?"

"I love it," Pat said truthfully, and then surprised herself by telling this very young Mrs. Corrick her fears about living in a tent. Now she could laugh about those fears herself.

"You may be lonesome here until school starts in the fall," Mrs. Corrick said thoughtfully. "All the children on the Base right now are a lot younger than you."

She stood up and put the placid baby over her shoulder.

"Let's be good neighbors," she suggested, smiling again. "Come over to see me every day, will you? If you like babies, you can have fun with Spuds. He's pretty nice."

Patricia loved babies and said so. She also liked this particular baby's pretty mother. From the doorway she watched the two of them go down the street and up their own walk; then alone again, she found that she had absolutely nothing to do. She tried the new piano, but she didn't know many pieces by heart, and of course she had no music here. She turned on the television and flipped the knobs from station to station, but couldn't find a program that interested her. She went hopefully to the bookshelves, but they contained only a few volumes about airplanes and one about military tactics, whatever they might bet.

When Robert came in to tell her that lunch was ready, it seemed like an exciting event.

"But my father isn't home yet, Robert."

"Major never can come for lunching. Too bad."

After lunch Patricia went into her bedroom and threw herself across the bed. Lying on her stomach with her chin on her hands, she stared out of the window at the little piece of green lawn and the trunk of the big pepper tree that it framed. If only she had some of her things here, she thought, miserably, her paper dolls, her storybook dolls, her music, her books. Surely Aunt Sue and Aunt Mary would think to put them in her trunk. Suddenly a spasm of homesickness seized her. She put her head down on her arms and cried as though her heart were breaking. Indeed she thought that it was breaking.

"I'm going home right away," she sobbed. "If my trunk comes today as Father said it would, I won't even open it. I can't stay here—I just simply can't."

Worn-out from crying, she fell asleep, and was awakened finally by her father's voice calling:

"Where's my girl?"

"Here," Patricia answered, wide awake at once. She thought determinedly—I'll go right out and tell him that I want to start back on the train tonight.

With hope in her eyes, she marched out into the living room. Her father came to meet her with a strange sort of smile that made her feel funny. He took her chin in his hand and turned her face up so that he could look into her eyes. Before she could speak, he said gravely:

"Do you know, Pat, this has been one of the longest days I've ever spent. I've looked at my watch at least a dozen times, waiting until time to come home. You see, I've really been waiting for seven years to have my own house and my own daughter—"

Tell him, Pat commanded herself furiously, tell him that you want to start back to Middleport tonight.

But she couldn't tell him—the words just simply wouldn't come.

Patricia's trunk didn't come that day, nor did it arrive the next morning. Without it, her clothes situation was becoming rather desperate. She had with her only the thing in which she had traveled, and another dress, the changes of underwear that she had brought in her suitcase, her pink kimono, and two pairs of pajamas.

She was accustomed to wearing fresh clothes every day, and that second morning after breakfast she eyed herself with distaste. She took her traveling dress from the closet but found that it looked just as bad as the one she had on. Suddenly it occurred to her that she could wash her clothes. She loved to wash things, and it would be something to do to pass the time.

She filled the basin in the bathroom with warm, sudsy water, washed her clothes, and rinsed them in the shining bathtub. While she was doing it, she thought she might as well wash her other things, too. She slipped out of the things she was wearing, put on her kimono, and washed them thoroughly. Both pairs of pajamas went into the improvised washtub, as well. Feeling pleased with herself, Patricia wrung all the garments out as well as she could and rolled each article up into a neat little bundle as she had seen Cora do many times. She had just finished and was beginning to wonder how well she could iron her clothes, when Robert tapped on her bedroom door.

"Miss Corrick on telephone," he called. "Wants Miss Pat should go to her house for lunching."

"Oh, tell her I'd love to," called back Pat, skipping to the door.

Then all of a sudden she realized what she had done—that she had washed every single piece of wearing apparel that she had brought with her except the pink kimono! For a moment she didn't know whether to laugh or cry. Opening the door a crack, she called down the hall to Robert, who was on his way back to the telephone, "Oh, Robert, I can't go. I can't possibly go. Please tell Mrs. Corrick I'm awfully sorry."

"Good for you to go," Robert protested, turning around.

"But I can't!" wailed Patricia.

39

"Miss Pat sick?"

"No. Oh, no!" gasped Pat, shaking with laughter.

It didn't seem quite so funny when she realized that she was a prisoner in her room with nothing to do. When she had recovered a little from the shock of her predicament, she remembered that she had writing paper and a pencil, and decided to write a letter to the aunts. It would be the longest letter she had ever written, she thought. It might very well turn out to be the longest letter that anyone had ever written, for she certainly had a good many hours ahead to devote to it.

She had filled a page and a half when she heard Robert go down the hall. She scrambled to the door and opened it.

"Robert, do we have a clothesline?"

"No clothesline," Robert said cheerfully. "Send everything to very good laundry. Miss Pat sick?"

"I never felt better," said Miss Pat.

Her clothes would certainly never dry, all rolled up in little bundles, she thought. She went to the bathroom, shook out the clothes, draped them over the towel racks and the edge of the bathtub, and returned to her letter.

After a long time Robert came to her door again.

"Lunching ready, Miss Pat."

Patricia was hungry, very hungry. She said wistfully, "Robert, would it be too much trouble for you to bring me a tray with my lunch on it?"

"Miss Pat sick?"

"NO!" shouted Patricia.

"I bring tray," Robert said hastily and departed.

When he returned, Patricia was sitting up in bed in her kimono, the sheet pulled up over her knees. Robert put the tray down on her lap.

"Miss Pat sick," he said firmly.

"Really and truly I'm not," Patricia declared. "I—I like to have lunch in bed sometimes."

She couldn't bring herself to tell him that she had washed all of her clothes at the same time—it was too silly.

She was just finishing a very good lunch when through the open window came the sound of a car stopping and someone coming up the walk. Then Pat heard her father's voice. He was talking with Robert and she wondered how he happened to be home at this time of day. In a moment or two he came back to her room.

"Robert says you're sick," he told her.

"I'm not the least bit sick," Patricia giggled.

"Well, I must say you don't look it," her father agreed, gazing with puzzled eyes at a perfectly well daughter having her lunch in bed. "If you're through eating, how about getting up and getting dressed now like a good girl? I have to drive to Santa Monica on business, and you may go with me and have your first sight of the ocean."

"Oh, goody, goody!" cried Pat, setting aside the tray and jumping out of bed. Then she remembered and stood stock-still, tears springing to her eyes.

"I can't get dressed," she said sadly. "All my clothes were dirty, and I washed them. Every single one of them—my anklets and my panties, every single thing except my kimono!"

"How extremely fortunate that you didn't wash that, too," Major Lowell said solemnly, then he and Patricia both began to laugh at the same second. Finally he said, with disappointment in his voice, "It's really tough, though, Pat. I thought we'd have a fine afternoon. Haven't you really anything at all to wear?"

"Not a thing," mourned Pat.

For the past few minutes they had both been vaguely aware of something going on at the front door. Now Robert came along the hall with his quick little steps.

"He come," he announced. "He so big can hardly climb through front door. Men bring him now."

Down the hall came two men, bearing Aunt Sue's largest wardrobe trunk. Pat took one look and began to jump up and down.

"I'll be ready to go to Santa Monica in five minutes," she sang joyfully. "On the way there may we please stop somewhere to buy a clothesline? I just can't keep house without a clothesline!"

AN ENCOUNTER WITH A GENERAL

THE trip to Santa Monica was wonderful. In the first place, after leaving the Base, Patricia had her first daylight glimpse of Frankfort, the bustling little city on the outskirts of which the Base had been built.

"You'll go to school in Frankfort," her father said. "The first day that I have time, I'll show you the school. It's just four or five blocks from the Base gates."

I won't be here when school begins, Patricia started to say, and again could not bring forth the words. Why, she thought, they couldn't start school in the old red-brick building in Middleport without her! She would be in sixth grade this fall and had been looking forward to having Miss Davis, the nicest teacher in the whole school. No, she certainly wouldn't be in California when it was time for school to open.

She forgot schools and home alike when her father, his business in Santa Monica completed, drove down to the beach, and the sea lay before her, blue, rolling, white-capped, magnificent. When the car stopped, she jumped out and ran to the water's edge, so excited that she could hardly breathe, the fresh salt wind in her hair, on her face, whipping her skirt. The waves breaking against the sand thundered and whispered, thundered and whispered.

"Why didn't anyone ever tell me what it is like?" Patricia cried to her father, who had come to stand beside her.

"It's one of the things that can't be told," Major Lowell smiled.

She felt that she couldn't bear it when at last they had to go, and was only a little consoled by the shells she had gathered to take back with her.

"We'll come back just as often as we can," her father promised.

The next morning Patricia unpacked her trunk and put her things away. Her familiar belongings gave her many a pang of homesickness, but it was fun to arrange them in their new places. The aunts had remembered to send all of her treasures, even her paints and crayons. They had sent two new dresses, too, a dark-blue dotted Swiss with white daisies appliquéd around its flaring skirt, and a white linen with coral buttons all the way down the front. Of course Patricia took time out from unpacking to try on the new frocks and to survey herself in the long mirror on the closet door. She wished that the girls at home could see her with her hair short. I don't look like Patricia any more, she thought. Pat suits me much better now.

That afternoon she spent a long time at the piano, pleased to have her music again. When her fingers grew tired, she took her dolls out into the patio to play with them there. The patio was a wonderful place in which to play, she thought. It was cool and quiet, and no strange dogs could wander in. Aunt Mary and Aunt Sue were nervous about dogs, and so of course Patricia was, too. The afternoon passed so quickly that she was surprised when her father came home.

"We're invited over to the Corricks' for dinner to-night," he told her, so Patricia gathered up her dolls and went to change her dress, delighted at having an opportunity to wear the new white linen dress so soon. With white anklets and slippers to complement the dress, she skipped into the living room where her father was waiting.

"I'd like to walk you all over the Base so that everyone here could see how nice you look," her father declared, as they started out.

Patricia smiled her thanks, then drew close to him as a big police dog crossed the road toward them.

"Don't look at him!" she commanded, her voice a bit shaky.

"Don't look at whom?" inquired her astonished parent.

"At that awful dog. I've found out that if you pretend you don't see dogs, they usually don't pay any attention to you, but if you even look at them, they're liable to come right up to you."

"Dogs are usually eager to make friends," the major remarked, and added, "I take it you don't like dogs."

"Oh, no. I'm really afraid of them, I guess," Patricia admitted.

"Have you ever had one of your own?"

"Good gracious, no!"

By that time they were going up the walk to the Corrick house and Captain Corrick was coming to meet them. Patricia was glad to find that he was young and attractive and nice. Young Spuds certainly was in luck with his parents. Patricia was disappointed at first to find that the baby was in bed and asleep, but right away she began to have so much fun that she fogot all about him. Captain Corrick led her and her father right out to the kitchen where Mrs. Corrick was bustling about with things on the stove. She greeted them gaily without stopping her stirring. In Middleport, when one was invited out to dinner, one sat decorously in the living room until summoned to the dining room; here, it seemed, everyone helped get dinner. Major Lowell set the table, Pat and Captain Corrick made lettuce and tomato salads on little plates, and they all carried food and dishes to the table. After dinner everyone helped clear the table and wash and wipe the dishes.

The laughter grew so noisy that Pat asked anxiously, "Won't we wake Spuds?"

"Goodness, no," Mrs. Corrick assured her, "an Air Force baby learns to sleep through everything."

The evening simply flew—Pat couldn't believe it when her father said that it was nine o'clock.

It had been a nice evening, she thought. Strolling home with her father was nice, too. Without even thinking about it, she slipped her small hand into his big one, and he looked down at her and smiled.

"Liking it here, Pat?"

"Yes. Father, were you awfully lonely after you brought me back from China?"

"Pretty lonely. You've no idea how I hated to give you over to the aunts, but I couldn't take a baby all over the world with me. I can't begin to tell you how happy I was when I knew that I was to be stationed here in the United States, and realized that you had grown old enough to be the lady of the house."

Patricia thought uneasily, I'm awfully afraid that

Father won't think that the whole summer is long enough.

The other nights that Pat had been sleeping in her new room she had been so tired that she had fallen asleep at once, but tonight sleep wouldn't come. For the first time she was aware of the sounds of the motors of planes. The planes seemed to be going around and around the Base. Maybe the pilots want to land and can't find the airfield, she thought uneasily.

She got out of bed and went over to the window to peer out into the night. There was no moon.

Those pilots will never be able to land, she thought worriedly. I wonder if Father has heard them up there. Perhaps he could do something to help them.

She put on her slippers and robe and went out to the living room where her father was reading the newspaper. He put it down when he heard her footsteps.

"Something the matter, Pat?"

"Not with me, but I'm afraid that those airplanes have got stuck up there. I mean they've stayed out after dark, and now how can they possibly get down safely?"

Major Lowell stood up, holding out his hand for hers.

"Come along outdoors, and I'll explain to you," he said. Wonderingly Pat went with him out to the patio.

"Now watch the sky," her father said. "In just a second you'll see a beam of light. There it is—see?"

"No— Where? Oh, yes, I do. Why it seems to be coming up from the ground and it's sweeping the sky, sort of, and circling the sky. Why, for goodness' sakes!"

"That's the beacon light," her father said. "It's located on the landing field and it circles the sky all night every night. Pilots can see it from miles and miles away on a clear night and it guides them in."

"Like a lighthouse guiding ships," Pat exclaimed.

"Exactly," said her father. He went on talking as he drew her into the house out of the cool night air. "When men first began flying at night, they were dependent upon the beacon, but now the modern planes do what we call instrument flying. The pilots can't get lost even if the night is so cloudy or so stormy that they can't see the field lights. I don't suppose you've ever heard about instrument flying, have you?"

"I don't know a single thing about it," Pat replied.

"Well, this is the way it works. Every air base and airport has what is called a control tower. The men who work in the tower are in radio contact all the time with the men in the planes. The planes receive their directions from two radio beams, and the pilot receives his flying instructions from a needle on the panel of his plane. If his needle is kept on zero, the beams will guide him right to the field, so if he's flying on instruments, he watches that needle all the time, just the way I watch the road when I'm driving the car. If the needle swings to the right, the pilot turns to the right until the needle goes back to zero. If the needle goes to the left, the pilot turns to the left until the needle again goes to zero. Do you understand?"

"No," said Pat, shaking her head. "I know it does because you say it does. But I don't understand it. I don't understand how a radio works or how television works, or anything about electric lights or the telephone. I don't even understand how a camera takes pictures. Do you suppose I will when I'm grown up?"

"Perhaps a little better than you do now," her

father said, laughing, as Pat kissed him good night and ran off to bed again, glad that the pilots of the planes had something to help them find the way down from the sky even if she couldn't understand it.

The following Monday Pat began her music lessons, with Mrs. Corrick teaching her. Mrs. Corrick had studied to be a concert pianist before she was married. She had offered to "trade" lessons for the privilege of using the Lowell piano, because the Corricks didn't have one.

"Of course we would be glad to have her practice on our piano at any rate," Major Lowell said to Pat, "but she really wants to teach you."

So Pat had her lessons while Spuds played contentedly on a blanket spread for him on the living-room floor. Pat was surprised at the progress she made. Often when she was practicing, Mrs. Corrick, who had heard the piano, would come in with Spuds under one arm, park him on the blanket, and sit down on the piano bench with Pat to help her with a difficult passage. Practicing with Mrs. Corrick wasn't work—it was fun, and when Mrs. Corrick herself played the piano, Pat would sit curled up on the davenport for an hour or more at a time listening to her. Pat had never heard such beautiful music as Mrs. Corrick's. It seemed that there must be magic in the tips of her slender fingers. I'm going to play like that someday, Pat promised herself.

The hours of each day, and the days themselves began to scurry by. When Pat tried to write to the aunts of what she had been doing, it seemed that she really hadn't been doing much, and yet she was busy all the time. She liked to spend the mornings playing in the front yard from where she could watch the activities of the Base. All the officers passing on the way to the Administration Building up the street seemed to know her and her father, and talked to her cheerily. The nurses on their way to the hospital were gay and friendly, too. They seldom had time to stop, but Pat often walked down to the hospital with a little group of them, and came to think of them as her friends. The young enlisted men who went by on motorcycles or in jeeps or command cars always waved to her or saluted her. She liked to watch the men drilling on the parade ground across the street; often the splendid Base band drilled there, and when it did, wild horses couldn't have dragged Pat off the front step.

She came to know most of the officers' wives, too. She liked to roller-skate back and forth on the long, level walk, and as she passed the different houses, someone often came out of one of them to talk with her, or to call her in to have some freshly baked cookies or a piece of cake. She liked seeing the interiors of the houses, for most of the officers and their wives had brought back interesting things from the foreign countries in which they had been stationed.

Pat's father worried, though, because there were no boys or girls her own age on the Base.

"But you'll make lots of friends when you start going to school," he said several times.

Whenever he said that, Pat felt uneasy. I should start thinking up some bad things to do, she reflected. Father likes to have me here, I know he does; I just must start doing naughty things so that he won't like to have me.

The trouble was that she simply couldn't think of anything naughty to do, no matter how hard she tried. She remembered the things her aunts wanted her to do or didn't want her to do. The aunts always insisted that she wash her hands before she went to the table for a meal.

I suppose it would be naughty to go to the table with awfully dirty hands, she thought, not very naughty, but at least a little bit naughty, for a start.

Just before dinner that night she went out to the flower borders and pulled a few weeds. All the time her father was serving her plate at the table, she thought about how dirty her hands felt. She put them on the table and looked at them. Yes, they were very, very dirty.

"Have you hurt your hands?" her father asked.

"Oh, no," Pat said, and then added hastily, with burning cheeks, "Father, may I please be excused for a moment?"

"Why, certainly."

Pat ran to the bathroom and scrubbed and scrubbed her hands. She just couldn't bear to handle food with dirty hands.

The thing is that Father and Robert let me do everything I want to do, and I don't want to do any naughty things, she thought, going back to the table.

Since there were no boys or girls her age on the Base, Pat played with the younger children and had quite a lot of fun doing it, cutting out paper dolls for them, making doll clothes, trying to fix broken toys, occasionally baby-sitting for a while when a mother had to go to the Post Exchange to do some errands.

If I were going to be here very long, I would just have to have some friends my own age, she thought, but it won't matter for this one summer.

Pat liked to skate very fast all the way up the street to General Chandler's house on the corner. She had never seen the general, but she wanted to, and always kept a watchful eye for him. Robert had taught her Air Force insignia, so she was sure she would recognize a general if she saw one.

Finally, one morning the general came out of his house just as Pat was skating by. She was skating pretty fast, but so anxious was she to look at him that she wheeled to a stop quickly, too quickly. The wheels of her skates caught together and down she went, practically under the general's feet. For one awful second she thought that she had upset him, too.

"Good gracious, child, are you hurt?" the general asked, leaning over to look at her in great consternation.

"I—I don't think so, thank you, sir," Pat stammered.

"Your knee is bleeding—you must have fallen on that stone."

Pat realized then that her knee was hurting pretty badly. She looked at it and felt a little sick.

"It looks as though all my blood is coming out," she said fearfully.

"We'll make sure that it doesn't," General Chandler said.

He looked around on the ground, picked up a stick, whipped a large clean handkerchief from his pocket, and in a jiffy had a tourniquet tight around Pat's leg.

"That's a good job as far as it goes," he said, with a pleased look at his handiwork, "but I think the wound should have professional care."

He leaned down and unfastened her skates and put them under the hedge, and, before Pat had even an inkling of what he intended to do, picked her up in his arms.

"Where are we going?" she gasped, hanging on

tightly, for the general was very tall, and she felt as though she were miles up in the air.

"I'm going to take you to the hospital across the street to have someone there clean and bandage that cut."

Pat was scared clear down to her bones.

"I thought people just went to hospitals to get babies or to have operations," she faltered, and the general chuckled.

"This is the Base hospital for casualties, and you're certainly a casualty," he told her.

"I'm getting blood all over your perfectly beautiful uniform," Pat wailed in distress.

"All in the line of my duty," the general said cheerfully.

He paused at the street intersection to look up and down before crossing it. An orderly, passing in a jeep, nearly ran his machine into a telephone pole in his amazement at seeing the Commanding Officer of the Base standing there with his arms full of Patricia.

Their arrival at the hospital caused a flutter, too. Doctors and nurses seemed to appear from everywhere to find out what General Chandler might want. One of the doctors took Pat out of the general's arms and strode down the hall with her. Looking over the doctor's shoulder with anxious eyes, Pat was relieved to see that the general was marching determinedly after them. She felt that he, at this moment, was her only friend. Once in the doctor's consulting office, she lost all of her fear and began almost to enjoy herself, because the doctor and the attendant nurse were both so nice and so gentle.

The doctor washed the cut carefully, and then Pat heard him speak horrible words.

"Iodine, nurse."

"Iodine, doctor."

At home, Pat always succeeded in persuading Aunt Mary or Aunt Sue to use nice, unhurting Mercurochrome on her scratches and skinned knees. At home, she would have howled at the mere suggestion of iodine.

"This is going to hurt," the doctor said in a kindly voice.

"I know it," Pat answered sadly.

She gripped the arms of her chair, closed her eyes, and set her teeth. For a moment she thought she must have been struck by lightning, but she wouldn't cry—she wouldn't even whimper.

"Good girl," said the doctor. The general, who had turned his back when the bottle of iodine appeared, muttered:

"You're a better soldier than I am. I'd raise the roof if anyone poured iodine on me like that."

Bandaged and on her feet again, Pat found that her knee didn't hurt much, and was only a little stiff. She walked out of the hospital with the general, and on the steps he asked her:

"Has the major taken you out to the flying field yet?"

"Just once," Pat answered, and then she added in astonishment, "Do you know who I am?"

"Certainly I know who you are," said the general, looking down at her with twinkling eyes. "I know that you were born in China, that you have lived with your aunts in Iowa since you were three years old, and that Madge Corrick is giving you piano lessons."

They laughed together, and then the general said, "I have to go out to the field right now. Would you like to go with me? I think your father is out there this morning—you may see him take up a ship."

Of course Pat wanted to go.

"In my car or in a jeep?" the general asked, his eyes twinkling more than ever.

"Oh, in a jeep, please," breathed Pat joyfully.

The two of them stood on the curb, and the general flagged down a jeep as one would flag a taxicab in the city. He and Pat climbed up into the tiny seat behind the surprised, sun-tanned young driver, and were off. Pat sat up just as straight as the general did, and she thought, giggling inside, that they must look awfully funny, she and General Chandler, sitting so dignified in the roaring, stubby little machine.

The size of the flying field and the great cavelike hangars took her breath away, as they had the first time she had seen them. Until she had seen that field and all its activities, she hadn't known that there were so many planes in the world—planes on the ground and in the air, planes landing and planes taking off.

The jeep stopped in front of the control tower building and the general got out.

"I won't be long," he told Pat. "You stay right where you are, young lady. I don't want to lose you out here."

Pat was more than willing to stay where she was. She had no desire to go closer to those noisy planes. The young driver of the jeep was from Des Moines . . . she found when she began to get acquainted with him. He and Pat had a fine time telling each other how much they liked Iowa. He pointed out different types of planes to her, and Pat was doing very well at learning to identify some of them herself when the general reappeared and climbed in beside her again.

"Your father's up on a flight," he told her.

Pat asked a little anxiously, "General Chandler, is flying very dangerous?"

"Not with a fine pilot like your father at the controls. As a matter of fact, we have very few accidents here, considering the number of ships we have in the air all the time."

Pat and the general parted on the warm terms of two good friends that day and they became better friends as time went on. Pat often met him outside his house, and skated along beside him to talk with him. He always made her hold his hand—he said that roller skating made him nervous! Pat thought it was awfully amusing that a general who wasn't afraid of planes and guns and wars should be nervous about roller skates.

One day General Chandler took her into the house to meet Mrs. Chandler, and after that Pat included the Chandler house in her almost daily round of neighborhood calls, for she liked Mrs. Chandler. She and the general had three grownup children, and five grandchildren, including one granddaughter just exactly Pat's age.

THE SURPRISE PACKAGE

THE breakfast bacon was crisp and delicious, the buttered toast was brown and crunchy, the orange juice was sweet and cold. Every bit of the breakfast was just the way Pat liked it, but she wasn't hungry. She pushed the bacon around on her plate, nibbled at the toast, and took a few very tiny sips of the orange juice.

"No appetite this morning?" her father asked, putting down the morning paper, headlines of which he had been scanning.

"Not much," Pat admitted.

"Feel bad anywhere?"

Pat hesitated before she spoke. Finally she said, raising her eyes to her father's, "I don't feel sick, but I don't feel just right."

"Something worrying you?"

"N-no. Well, yes, I suppose something is."

"Care to tell me about it?"

Again Pat hesitated before answering. She looked out through the open window of the dining room, out into the beautiful blue and green California world, and sighed sharply.

"You see," she said earnestly, looking back to her father, "it's just that I've done everything that there is to do here, and I just don't know what in the world I'm going to do this whole long day, or tomorrow, or the next day—"

Her father's eyes looked so sad that Pat wished she hadn't spoken the words, although she did feel bad, very bad indeed, so bad that she was afraid she might begin to cry at any minute.

"Of course you're homesick," her father said, in a matter-of-fact tone. "I felt sure that you would be when the newness of the Base had worn off."

"What do people do about homesickness?" Pat asked. She was ashamed of the little quaver in her voice and tried to smile, but didn't succeed very well.

"The thing to do is to keep busy."

"That's just it. I haven't anything to DO!" Pat said, the tears squeezing themselves out of her eyes.

Major Lowell looked at her regretfully, then glanced at his wristwatch and got up quickly from his chair.

"I've got to dash along, Pat," he said. "I wish I could stay home for a while to try to cheer you up but I can't. I have to fly a jetplane to San Pedro, and I won't be home until dinnertime. But I'll tell you something that may cheer you—yesterday I ordered a surprise for you delivered this morning. Try to keep your chin up until it comes, will you?"

"What is it?" Pat asked, diverted.

She left the table as he did and walked along with him out of the house and toward the garage.

"It's something you'll have fun with," Major Lowell

58

promised. "When I was your age, I couldn't have got along without one."

"Is it a big thing or a little thing or a middle-sized thing?"

"Big," said Major Lowell, hurrying along the flower-bordered walk.

"Is it animal, vegetable, or mineral?" Pat called after him, as he outdistanced her.

"Mineral. Good-by now. I'm sure that the surprise will really make a big difference."

Pat stood in the sunny yard to watch her father back the car out of the garage. She waved good-by to him and watched the car out of sight down the street.

I don't see how any big mineral thing could make me feel not homesick, she thought, and went around to the kitchen door to ask Robert whether he knew what the surprise was.

Robert didn't know, and as he was about to start using the vacuum cleaner on the rugs in the front rooms, he didn't seem to want to help Pat try to guess what it might be.

Pat went into her own room and stood for a moment looking around it.

It is a pretty room, she thought, feeling oddly dissatisfied with it, but it isn't nearly so pretty as my room at home.

She made her bed, jerking the sheets and spread into place. The more she jerked the spread, the worse it looked.

I don't care how the old bed looks, she thought, glaring at it.

She gave the spread one final pull, made a face at the bed, and then looked around for something else to do. She might dust the furniture, she supposed, but she didn't want to. What was the use? It would just get dusty again in no time.

She walked down the hall and into the living room where Robert was vacuuming away at a great pace. She could tell by the way he was opening and shutting his mouth that he was singing, but she couldn't hear his voice over the noise of the machine.

I'll bet he can't even hear himself, she thought crossly. I think it's silly to sing when you can't even hear yourself.

She couldn't even practice while Robert was running the vacuum cleaner. She didn't want to practice anyhow.

I don't want to do anything but go home, she thought miserably, going out to sit on the front steps.

She looked up and down the street, hoping that someone or something interesting would come along. With her elbows on her knees and her chin in her cupped hands, she watched the traffic going by.

When I first came, I thought that jeeps were cute, she reflected. Now I don't think they're at all cute. They're ugly things.

She looked up at the brilliant blue sky, squinting under its brightness.

I'm tired of sunshine, she thought. Out here in California there's just nothing but sunshine all the time. I wish it would rain for two or three days in a row the way it does at home sometimes.

A delicate, slim trail of white against the turquoise blue of the sky caught and held her attention. The little ribbon of white meant that a jetplane was shooting along up there, she knew, faster than any train, faster than any wind, faster than almost anything.

Her eyes found the plane, a tiny speck in the heavens.

That's probably Father's plane, she thought. She began to feel in her stomach the uneasiness that she always had when she knew her father was flying.

"Statistics will show you that airplanes are the safest kind of transportation," Major Lowell had told her when she confided her fears to him.

In spite of statistics, whatever they are, I just don't think that it's safe for people to be so far off the ground, Pat thought.

The jetplane was gone from her sight in an instant. Watching the white trail in the sky until it, too, disappeared, Pat shivered, although it was warm in the sunshine.

A panel truck drove up and stopped in front of the house. While its driver sat peering at the house number, Pat thought with delight, here comes the surprise, and jumping to her feet, she ran down to the street.

"Do you have a package for Major Lowell?" she asked the driver, a tall, tired-looking man in well-worn overalls.

"Is this 610 Base Road?"

"Yes, it is. Are you bringing a package for me?"

"Well, I got something for Miss Patricia Lowell at 610 Base Road, but 'taint a package," the man said.

He got out of the truck on the street side, and went to the back of the truck to open the rear door.

"A big mineral thing not in a package," Pat chanted aloud to herself. Joining the man at the rear of the truck, she peered inside with lively interest.

There was nothing in the truck but a tire jack, a monkey wrench, an old, dusty tire, and a blue bicycle.

"Oh, dear, I guess you forgot the thing for me," Pat said unhappily.

"Guess I didn't," the man said.

With his long arms, he reached up for the bicycle.

The "thing" came out of the truck with a whirring front wheel. Pat drew back in alarm, but the man steadied the vehicle and eased it down onto the pavement. Having rested it against the rear right fender of the truck, he took a grimy paper and a broken yellow pencil from his pocket, and handed paper and pencil to Pat.

"Now then, little girl," he said, "if you'll sign here where it says 'Received by—' the bicycle will be all yours, and I'll be on my way."

"It can't be for me," Pat protested. "Why would a bicycle be coming for me? I don't want a bicycle."

"Well, you got one," the man said. "Just sign where it says 'Received by—' "

The truck driver frowned at Pat, and Pat frowned at him. Reluctantly she took the pencil, and signed her name on the paper. After all, the bicycle had been received by Patricia Lowell; there was no doubt about that.

The man put the bicycle bars into Pat's unwilling hands, slammed the rear door of the truck, got in behind the steering wheel and drove off.

"Thank you!" Pat shouted after him, belatedly remembering her manners.

She stood holding up the bicycle and looking at it in dismay.

This is the only present I've ever got in my whole life that I don't like, she thought.

She had never learned to ride a bicycle, and, what's more, she didn't want to learn. The only one of her friends who had a bicycle was Sally Fredericks, and last summer Sally had run into the side of a car and broken her leg. After that the parents who had been thinking about getting bicycles for their daughters had said "Absolutely no." Sally had been taken to the hospital and was unconscious for hours and hours. None of the girls really wanted a bicycle after Sally's accident.

"That's the surprise, I bet," Robert called from the front doorway.

"I bet it is, too," Pat answered sadly.

She couldn't spend the day standing in the street holding the thing up. Gingerly she took a step or two forward. The front wheel of the machine plunged sharply inward; the whole thing seemed to double up, with Pat on the inside of the V it made. She jerked the handlebars, lost her balance, and hit her left ankle viciously against a pedal. The pain brought tears to her eyes. She set her teeth and started to move forward, but the front wheel bumped hard against the high curb, bringing Pat and the bicycle to an abrupt stop.

"Lift wheel over curb," Robert called.

Feeling very silly because she hadn't thought of doing that herself, Pat managed to propel the unwelcome present over the curb and up to the steps. She let the bicycle fall to the ground then and bent to rub her aching anklebone.

"Very fine bicycle," Robert said. "You have fun now you got him. You know how to ride him?"

"No," sighed Pat.

"Pretty soon I finish in here, then I come and teach you. You learn very quick and surprise Major when he come home."

Robert went back into the house, and Pat looked at the bicycle. It had a wire basket across the front.

I could carry things in that if I had any things to carry, Pat thought.

She rang the bell of the bicycle several times. It gave forth a pleasant, polite little tinkle. It might be sort of fun to have a bicycle, she thought, feeling a sudden

63

quiver of excitement. If she could learn to ride the thing really well, she could get on it and go everywhere, except that there was really no place to go. She might find places, however.

No, she decided swiftly. She would never learn to ride the bicycle. If she did learn and did find places to go, her father would think that she was having a good time, he might make her stay. Besides, this gave her a splendid chance to be naughty. Her father wanted her to learn to ride, else he wouldn't have bought the bicycle for her. Well, she wouldn't learn to ride. She wouldn't thank him for the bicycle either; not thanking him for a present would be very rude and very naughty. If she were sufficiently rude and sufficiently naughty, he wouldn't want her here with him, and she could go home—home—home—

"Come on now, get on," Robert said from behind her. "I got time now to teach you."

"I really don't think I want to learn right now, Robert."

"Sure you do. Bicycle no good if you can't ride him. Major want you to ride him and have lots of fun."

"I really like to walk, Robert. I don't have to ride things, because I really enjoy walking."

"Go faster riding."

"But I don't need to go faster. If I have to go fast, I can run."

Robert looked at Pat, and Pat looked at Robert.

"Major be disappointed," he said firmly.

Pat's plan didn't include being rude to Robert, so she took a deep breath before she said, "Well, all right. Robert, if I get on that thing, will you hold me up and not let go for a single second?"

"Promise."

Robert steadied the bicycle, and Pat, feeling awk-

64

ward and helpless, got up on its seat and put her feet on the pedals. Just because I'm sitting on this thing I don't have to learn to ride it, she thought.

Up and down the street they went—Robert holding onto the handlebars, pulling in mightily when Pat over-balanced to the left, and bracing himself to help her keep her balance when she leaned to the right.

After a while Robert said breathlessly, "We stop now while I wipe perspiration off face."

Gratefully Pat slid off the bicycle and stood with her feet on the good, solid earth.

"I think that's enough for the first lesson," she said decidedly.

"Probably," Robert agreed, mopping his forehead with his handkerchief. "Maybe it go better when Major teach you."

To Pat's delight, Robert wheeled the bicycle off to the garage, and she was free to go into the house to wash her hot face and hands and get a cool drink of water.

All during that long day, Pat found herself thinking about the bicycle and worrying about her plan not to thank her father for it.

But I AM going to be rude, she told herself over and over again. I've just got to do something to make Father send me home.

Underneath the worry about the bicycle was the other worry, almost like a pain, that she always had when she knew that her father was flying.

Her heart lifted when she heard her father drive the car into the garage shortly before dinnertime, and then sank again when she thought of the conversation that she must have with him about the bicycle.

"Well, I see the bicycle came," Major Lowell said with a happy smile, when he found Pat waiting for him at the door. "Have you been having fun with it today?"

Tell him NO, Pat ordered herself. She heard herself saying hurriedly:

"I—I was so surprised when the man brought it."

"Do you like it, Pat?"

Tell him NO, Pat commanded herself. She said feebly:

"I— Well, it's a very nice color. And oh, I do like the bell. It's—it's such a pleasant-sounding bell."

Major Lowell looked at her sharply before he spoke.

"What's wrong with the bicycle, honey?"

"Oh, there's nothing wrong with it. Really and truly there isn't. It's just about the nicest bicycle I ever saw."

"Then what is the matter?"

"Well, you see, I don't know how to ride it."

"You'll learn in no time," her father said, so cheerfully that Pat thought he didn't even realize how rude she was.

Under the circumstances, she doubted very much that she would learn to ride in "no time," as he had predicted.

The next morning, about half-past eight, after a long hour spent trying to teach Pat to balance herself on the handsome blue bicycle, Major Lowell also began to doubt that his daughter would ride it.

It had been a very bad hour for Pat. Even if I wanted to learn to ride, I don't think I could, she thought. It wasn't too bad while her father was walking along beside her holding the handlebars, though her legs did get awfully tired going up and down, up and down with the pedals; but it was dreadful when he let go and told her to go along by herself. The instant he took his hands away from the bars, the front wheel began to wobble, and in about thirty seconds Pat's feet left the pedals to bump along the sidewalk. Before long she

66

and bicycle came to a tangled stop that was almost a fall.

When her father had to leave to go to the airfield, Pat went into the house with flushed cheeks and aching legs. Robert looked at her sympathetically.

"Hard to learn," he said kindly. "I help you after you rest a little."

"Father's going to give me another lesson after dinner tonight," Pat said wearily. "Until then, I just want to forget all about it." .

She made no progress during the evening lesson and none during the lesson the next morning. At the conclusion of that third lesson, Major Lowell looked at his daughter thoughtfully.

"Pat, do you really want to learn to ride?" he asked.

Pat's hot face grew even hotter. She hesitated, but she could only give him an honest answer.

"No," she said sadly.

"Why not, Pat?"

Pat couldn't meet his eyes with their tender, affectionate look, and she couldn't speak because of the lump in her throat. She closed her eyes and shook her head.

"Very well," Major Lowell said soberly, but not crossly, "I'll put the bicycle in the garage, and we'll just leave it there for the time being. Perhaps sometime you'll want to ride it."

Pat ran into the house thinking, when I get home I'm never, never going to be naughty again in all my life —I'm never even going to think a naughty thought.

OLD TODD HUNTER

THE same week that Pat became the owner of a bicycle, Todd Hunter arrived on the Base. He and his father, Captain Hunter, and his mother came to live in the house four doors away from the Lowell house.

Early in the morning of the day the Hunters arrived, Robert said to Patricia:

"New captain here with family down the street. Moving van in front of house. Maybe got some children."

"Oh, maybe, maybe, maybe!" Pat sang, running outdoors to look down the street.

Two men were carrying chairs and tables and a barrel from the van into the house. While Pat watched, one of the men took a dilapidated yellow bicycle from the van and stood it up on the grass in front of the house. Almost instantly, a thin, wiry, dark-haired boy, about Patricia's height, burst from the house and jumped onto the bicycle. Patricia watched in fascination, while he circled the house three times, then rode down the terrace, and went zooming off down the sidewalk, very fast, standing up on the pedals, and pumping for dear life. Pat had never seen anyone ride as fast as the boy was riding.

All of a sudden she remembered that it wasn't polite to watch the activities of one's neighbors. Reluctantly she went back into the house, got her writing materials, and took them to the patio to compose a letter to the aunts.

"Dear Aunt Mary and Aunt Sue," she began, "This morning a boy came to live on our street. I think he's about my age—"

That seemed to be about all she had to say to the aunts at that moment. She couldn't tell them how homesick she was, because knowing that she was unhappy would make them unhappy.

She sat chewing the eraser on her pencil and thinking about the boy. She had never played with boys because there were none near her age in the neighborhood at home.

She tried to think what games boys played. Baseball—football— As she thought of the boys she knew in school, she remembered that almost all of them always carried some kind of ball and toy guns.

I'm afraid a boy won't be much good to me, she decided regretfully.

Just then she heard a bicycle bell ringing out by the kitchen door and a boy's voice saying to Robert, "Where's the girl who lives in this house?"

Pat dropped her writing pad and pencil and rushed to the kitchen. Robert stood in the doorway, looking out at the boy, who stood astride his yellow bicycle, his dark eyes very bright and alert.

Pat slipped around in front of Robert and looked at the boy with as much interest as he was looking at her.

"How did you know I lived here?" she demanded.

"Saw a girl's bicycle in the garage as I rode by," the boy said airily. "My name's Todd Hunter, and I'm eleven. How many kids are there on the Base?"

"There's only me and some babies."

"Gosh," Todd Hunter said with great emphasis and then added, "I sure wish you were a boy."

"Well, I certainly wish you were a girl," Pat snapped.

Robert interposed soothingly, "There now—there now—" but Todd Hunter threw back his head and laughed.

"Well, anyhow," he said, "get on your wheel and come show me what there is to see on this Base."

"I can't ride the bicycle," Pat said, somehow feeling ashamed.

"What's the matter? You got a broken leg or something?"

"Of course I haven't got a broken leg. I just don't know how to ride, that's all."

"You've got a bicycle and don't know how to ride it? Well, for Pete's sake. Well, so long. I can find the way around by myself anyhow."

Todd was off like a streak.

"Now you have someone to play," Robert said to Pat, looking pleased.

"Well, maybe," Pat answered doubtfully, "but I don't see how I can play with someone who just rides around and around and around on a bicycle."

She went back to the patio and picked up her pencil and writing pad. After a moment she put them down without having written a word, and went out to the garage.

There was the bicycle, blue and shining.

Pat rang its bell softly two or three times, then, sigh-

in the big room; not even the attendant was there at the moment.

She's probably gone out to lunch, Pat thought.

She put a dime into the telephone slot and carefully dialed the number of the Lowell house. After a moment she got a busy signal; she retrieved her dime when it came tumbling back and waited for what seemed a very long time before she dialed again. After the second dialing, she again heard the busy signal.

Oh, dear, oh, dear, oh, dear, she thought, distressed because Mrs. Lattimore must wait so long.

The third time Pat heard the busy signal she gave up.

It will only take us a few minutes to get to the Lattimore house, she thought. I'll telephone Robert from there. I'm simply not going to keep that nice Mrs. Lattimore waiting any longer.

The Lattimore house was one of a row of pretty residences with wide green lawns, big trees, and bright gardens. Pat liked it at once, because it seemed to be such a friendly house, with light-colored furniture and bright chintzes at the windows, with bowls of flowers on the tables, and books and magazines around in profusion.

When Pat and Aleathe went upstairs to wash their hands and faces before lunch, Pat found that the bathroom fixtures were pale green. She had never seen any kind but white ones before. She would have liked to stay in the bathroom a long time to admire the pretty fixtures, the pale-yellow walls and towels, but Aleathe hurried her along, because she had so many other things to show her.

"This is Mother's and Daddy's room," Aleathe said, pausing in the doorway of a big bedroom. "See all the perfume bottles on the dressing table? Those are my mother's. She's just crazy about perfume, so Daddy and I usually give her some for birthdays and Easter and Mother's Day. Would you like to smell some of the different kinds?"

Pat was enchanted with the lovely fragrances that were wafted from the bottles when the girls carefully removed the stoppers. At home, Aunt Mary had a bottle of what she called violet water, and Aunt Sue had a bottle of lilac water, but the contents of those bottles didn't smell nearly so good as did the contents of Mrs. Lattimore's perfume bottles.

"We can put some on us if we want to," Aleathe said. "Mother always lets me. I'm going to put on some Chanel No. 5 because that's my favorite. What do you choose?"

After some consideration, Pat selected Twilight Star, because she thought the name sounded like a poem.

"We'll put it behind our ears the way mother does," Aleathe said.

Pat was surprised to hear about putting perfume behind one's ears. The aunts always put their lilac water and violet water on their handkerchiefs.

"Mother won't care if I show you her lipsticks," Aleathe said, pulling open a little drawer in the dressing table to show an array of small, golden tubes. "Isn't it funny how women have so many different shades of lipstick to go with different-colored clothes? When I'm old enough to wear lipstick, I'm just going to have one at a time, then I won't have to be bothered trying to decide which one to use. They all look about alike to me, anyhow."

At home, neither Aunt Mary nor Aunt Sue nor Cora had even one lipstick. Here, Pat longed to open all the little tubes to see the different shades, but Aleathe was in a hurry to show Pat her own room, so Pat, resolving to have a big drawer just full of lipsticks when she grew up, had to follow her little hostess.

Aleathe's room, like Pat's in Iowa, was pink and white. Even her furniture was white. There was a big dollhouse in one corner of the room, and where there weren't windows in the walls, there were shelves filled with books and toys.

Aleathe was so eager to show Pat all her treasures that Mrs. Lattimore had to call the girls twice to come to lunch, but she wasn't cross about the delay. She just laughed about it, and said that getting acquainted with a new friend was more interesting and more important than eating lunch.

Pat and Aleathe had a long, happy afternoon together.

Aleathe was very generous with her possessions, insisting that Pat choose what dolls and paper dolls she wanted to have for her very own during the afternoon.

"They will be your very own whenever you come," she added.

The girls played together as though they had known each other all their lives. Although the thought made her feel somewhat disloyal, Pat decided that Aleathe was even more fun than Sally, her very favorite of all her good friends at home.

Although of course I still like Sally better than anybody, she thought quickly.

Pat and Aleathe could hardly believe it when Mrs. Lattimore came to the door of Aleathe's room and said it was five o'clock. If they didn't let Pat go home now, she laughed, perhaps her father wouldn't let her come again.

"Oh, Mother, we've had such fun," Aleathe said, getting reluctantly to her feet from the floor where the paper-doll families were spread out. "I wish Pat could live with us, so that we could play together all the time. I wish now that we didn't have to go away next week."

Pat's heart sank. All afternoon she had been thinking that the summer wouldn't seem very long now that she had found Aleathe.

"Aren't you going to live here any more?" she asked.

"Oh, yes, indeed," Mrs. Lattimore assured her. "We're going to take a long trip, though. We're leaving next Wednesday for Quebec, Canada, to spend the rest of the summer with Aleathe's grandparents."

"We'll play together every day before I go," Aleathe said, seeing Pat's disappointed expression.

"You and Aleathe will have lots of fun together after school opens in the fall," Mrs. Lattimore added.

"I won't be here then," Pat said. "I'm going back to Middleport to go to school there."

"Oh, I don't want you to! Please, please, please, don't!" Aleathe wailed.

Pat shook her head, smiling. She felt very much better now that she had said those words aloud instead of just thinking them, as she had been doing for so long.

The two girls and Mrs. Lattimore went out to the driveway to get into the car. Pat sat in the front seat between Aleathe and her mother. Then Pat asked:

"May Aleathe play at my house tomorrow? I know that Father would like to have me ask her to come for lunch."

"Certainly she may," Mrs. Lattimore answered, and Aleathe giggled.

To Pat's inquiring look Aleathe explained, "I'm laughing because you sound so grownup when you say

'Father' instead of 'Daddy.' I don't know any other girl who calls her daddy 'Father.' Why do you?"

"I suppose because I don't know him very well," Pat said.

She felt her cheeks grow hot. She felt hot inside of her, too, not because of Aleathe's gentle teasing, but because the conversation made her think again, as she had to think so many times, of her father's disappointment because she could not bring herself to use the word he wanted to hear. She could see that disappointment in his eyes almost every night when she met him as he drove in. Often, for his sake, she had tried to make herself say "Hi, Daddy," instead of "Hi, Father," but she couldn't do it. She just couldn't; the word just wouldn't come.

They rode along in silence for a short distance. Aleathe leaned forward to turn on the car radio; after a moment the music came, dancing music that made Pat's feet beat the time against the floorboard. Aleathe, who knew the words of the song, began to sing softly.

The music stopped suddenly, right in the middle of a measure. The announcer's voice broke in abruptly:

"Ladies and gentlemen, we are interrupting this program to bring you a special bulletin from our newsroom—"

"Oh, dear, I suppose something dreadful has happened," Aleathe said, sitting forward on the seat.

Pat's throat began to ache. Father, she thought. Could it be Father? Could there have been a plane crash?

"The little girl, missing from the country club grounds since before noon today, as previously reported to you, has not been found. I repeat, the little girl who disappeared from the country club before noon today has not been found—"

Well, anyhow, nothing has happened to Father thought Patricia, and relaxed.

"I wonder who—" said Mrs. Lattimore and Aleathe together, then stopped abruptly as the announcer's voice swept on, sounding hurried and excited.

"Anybody who has seen this child, a little girl, ten years old, with curly blond hair and gray eyes, when last seen wearing a white blouse, navy shorts, and tennis shoes—"

"That sounds like you," said Aleathe, looking at Pat wonderingly.

"It can't be me," Pat said, laughing. "I haven't disappeared. I'm right here."

The announcer went on. "If you have any information about this child, please call the police or headquarters at the air base immediately. Grave fears are felt for the child's safety. As we told you in our earlier broadcasts, the little girl's bicycle was found in the country club parking lot, where it is known she left it this morning, leading police officers to believe she may have been abducted. Police, sheriff's officers, and special detachments of the military from the air base are combing the town and countryside. I repeat, if anyone listening has any information about the whereabouts of Patricia Lowell, only child of Major Trent Lowell, please—"

Mrs. Lattimore swerved the car to the side of the road and stopped it, her face pale, her hands shaking, as Pat cried out:

"Why, that radio is talking about me!"

"But, Mother," Aleathe said in a shaky voice, "I don't understand why anyone should think that Pat has disappeared. She telephoned home to tell Robert that she was going home with us. Don't you remember she did, Mother? You did, didn't you, Pat?"

Of course I did, Pat started to say, and then she remembered.

"Oh, dear! Oh, dear! Oh, dear! I tried to call from the country club. I tried three times, but the line was always busy, and I didn't want to keep you waiting any longer, so I thought I would call as soon as I got to your house, only when I got there I forgot all about it, and I never thought of it again until just this minute. Oh, dear! Oh, dear! Oh, dear!"

"What shall we do, Mother?" Aleathe asked, beginning to cry.

"We'll get Pat home just as fast as we can," Mrs. Lattimore said, her voice shaking, too. "I'll take the back road—we can get there faster than we could find a telephone to make a call."

During the short, fast drive, the three sat in silence. Aleathe put her cold left hand on Pat's cold right hand, and held it tightly. Pat was grateful for the friendly gesture, but she was feeling so sick at heart that she could make no response.

In a matter of minutes, the car came to the gates of the Base, where a sentry stepped up to halt it, as he always halted all ingoing cars. Pat saw with surprise that Captain Blaine, the officer of the day, was with the sentry. She knew that officers of the day never stood sentry duty. Both Captain Blaine and the sentry were grim-faced and erect, as though they were in a war, Pat thought afterward when she was reliving the scene.

"I have Patricia Lowell with me," Mrs. Lattimore said crisply, "safe and sound. I'd like to take her to her father as quickly as possible."

"I'll go with you to show you the way," Captain Blaine said. "Airman Browne, see that the word gets to headquarters."

"Yes, sir," the young sentry said, saluting smartly, his sun-tanned face suddenly alight with a smile.

When they reached the Lowell house, Pat ran up the walk with Aleathe, Mrs. Lattimore and Captain Blaine following them. There were a good many people in the living room: General Chandler, Mrs. Chandler, Mrs. Corrick, some officers Pat didn't know, two policemen, and Robert. They were all walking around and around the room; no one was sitting down. From the doorway Pat's eyes at once found her father among all the people. She saw how white and worried he was.

"I haven't disappeared—I'm not missing," she cried, "I just forgot to telephone. Oh, Father, I'm so sorry—"

Then she was in her father's arms, and he was holding her so tight that she could scarcely breathe.

Much later, after explanations had been made over and over again, after Mrs. Lattimore and Aleathe and the neighbors and the officers had gone, after Robert had served dinner with hands that were still shaking because of his hours of anxiety, Pat said disconsolately to her father as she sat with him in the living room:

"You didn't eat a bite of dinner."

"I wasn't hungry, sweetheart."

"I would feel better about it if you would scold me dreadfully hard and punish me."

"You don't deserve a scolding or a punishment, dear. Forgetting isn't being naughty."

"The strange part of it is," Pat said thoughtfully, "when I was trying to be naughty, I couldn't be very bad. Now, when I am trying to be good, I did the worst thing I have ever done in all of my life."

"When were you trying to be naughty, and why?" Major Lowell asked in surprise.

Pat drew a quick breath of dismay. She had just been thinking—she hadn't really intended to say the words aloud. Since she had spoken them, though, there was nothing to do but explain them.

"I—I thought," she said, "that if I was very, very bad, you wouldn't want me to stay here with you and would let me go home. The trouble with that was, I couldn't find anything very bad to do, only little things, like saying 'gosh' because you didn't like the word, and not learning to ride my bicycle when you wanted me to, and not making my bed or dusting my room properly— But you never seemed to mind those things at all."

"I didn't even notice them," her father said. He was smiling at her, but in spite of the smile, he looked so sad that Pat wanted to cry. "I've thought all along that you've been remarkably good, really wonderfully good."

"I've been trying to be lately, since—"

"Since when, honey?"

"Ever since the day you told me that I may go home whenever I feel that I have to." Pat had to say it, although she didn't want to.

"I see," Major Lowell said.

After a long moment, he smiled at her again.

"It's long past your bedtime, Pat—better run along now. I'm glad that you've found a little girl with whom to be friends. I liked her, and I liked her mother."

Pat lay awake a long time that night, feeling sorry about all the worry she had caused her father and Robert and all of her friends on the Base. She had heard one of the policemen saying to the other as they were leaving, "That little miss ought to have a good paddling," and she agreed with him. How could she have been so thoughtless?

Trying to stop thinking about the dreadful thing

91

she had done, she began thinking about going home to Middleport, planning what she would wear on the homeward-bound train, wondering who would meet her at the Middleport station.

I'll be so happy when I get back, she thought.

Then she remembered how sad her father had looked when she told him her plan about being naughty, and she felt sad, too.

Even thinking and thinking about going home couldn't make her feel any more cheerful.

I guess you just can't be happy yourself unless the people around you are happy, she thought, and was glad to begin to feel sleepy at last.

PAT'S BIRTHDAY CELEBRATION

PAT had a contented and happy week with Aleathe before the Lattimores left for their trip to Canada. She and Aleathe played together all day every day, at the country club, at Pat's house, at Aleathe's house. They both liked to play everything exactly the same way, and they felt as though they had known each other all their lives. Very soon each was confiding her very most secret thoughts to the other.

Aleathe told Pat that she had been unhappy until she met Pat, because the girls in her crowd were talking about being too old to play with dolls, and laughing at her because that was all she ever wanted to do.

"Peggy Lee Anderson has put all her dolls and all her paper dolls in a box in her attic, and she says that she's never going to play with them again. Of course Peggy Lee is almost a year older than you and I are," Aleathe said. "I just couldn't do that to my dolls, ever.

I'm going to play with them until I go to junior high school."

"So am I," Pat declared. "I'll even play with them when I'm going to the great big high school, if I want to, and I think that I will want to—I'm practically sure that I will."

"Oh, I wish you were going to live here," Aleathe sighed. "Why won't you, Pat?"

So Pat told Aleathe about how much she loved the aunts and Cora and her home and her life in Middleport.

Aleathe listened gravely, and after a while she said thoughtfully, "I think that your daddy was right, though, when he told you that you and he should be together. I think that children should be with their parents. Anyhow, I don't see how you can bear to leave your daddy. I just love him. Next to my own daddy, he's the nicest one I ever met. Maybe he won't let you go home. What will you do if he says you can't go?"

"He's said that I may go if I feel that I just have to, and when it's time for school to begin, I will feel that I just have to," Pat said.

Then she told Aleathe all about trying to be naughty so that her father would send her home, and about how hard it was to find naughty things to do.

"Why, I should think that being naughty would be the easiest thing in the world," said Aleathe, who had listened in astonishment.

"Well, it isn't," Pat assured her. "You just try it sometime if you think it is. You can't do the really bad things like lying and stealing, you know, and as for the other things, well, Father was always willing for me to do the things I wanted to do, and the things he wouldn't have wanted me to do were the things I didn't want to do anyhow."

94

"Well, I'll bet I can think of plenty of naughty things to do," Aleathe said firmly. "I'm not going to try it while we're on our trip, but when we get home, I am certainly going to try it. I may not DO the naughty things, but I'll bet I can THINK of some."

The two girls felt very sad when they told each other good-by.

"We'll write to each other all of our lives, even when we're old, old women," they promised.

Pat was restless after Aleathe had gone. She had fun with the other children at the country club, but she didn't meet any with whom she wanted to be "best friends."

When her birthday drew near and she began to think about it, she felt that she didn't know any of the children well enough to invite them to a party. It would be the first birthday she could remember for which she hadn't had a party, she thought dismally.

Patricia's birthday was the twelfth of August.

At home, she and her aunts had planned and anticipated her birthday with almost as much excitement as they had anticipated Christmas. Days beforehand, the aunts would come home from shopping with delightful-looking packages that Patricia was happily sure contained just the things she wanted most. She always awoke on her birthday to a big pile of presents and a thrilling day of joy.

Here, however, no one had mentioned the nearness of her birthday. There was no delightful planning of a party, no packages were hidden away with much laughter and many false clues as to what they contained. Other years her father had always sent her lovely presents from whatever part of the world he happened to be in. Of course, coming from so far away, the packages had never arrived on the day itself.

Sometimes they came early, and sometimes they came late, but they always proved that her father had remembered her birthday well ahead of time.

Wondering upon what day of the week her birthday would fall this year, Patricia went out into the kitchen to ask Robert for a calendar.

"Not got calendar," Robert said regretfully.

"Oh, well, never mind. I can figure out what I want to know," Pat said. "What day of the month is this, Robert?"

"July thirty."

Pat went back into her room to do her figuring.

I wish I'd asked Robert how many days there are in July, she thought, sitting on the edge of her bed. Let me see—what's that old rhyme—"Thirty days hath September, April, June, and—and July"? That doesn't sound quite right.

She said the rhyme over to herself two or three times, and finally decided that she had it right. Well, then, tomorrow would be the first of August. It was hard to count that many days ahead. She counted Monday—Tuesday—Wednesday—Thursday several times and finally came to the conclusion that her birthday would be Wednesday of the week after next.

As the days passed and the birthday was not mentioned, she tried to comfort herself with the thought that Aunt Mary and Aunt Sue hadn't forgotten. She had had a letter from each of them that week, and each of them had written lovingly, "Soon you will be eleven years old, darling."

It isn't that I mind not having presents, Pat thought, trying to get to sleep the night of her birthday eve. As far as presents go, Aunt Mary and Aunt Sue are sure to send tons of things. It's just that it's so awful to think that on the day I'm eleven years old no one will even say "Happy birthday" to me.

It was a comfort, too, to think that very soon now she would be going back to Middleport. School always began the first week in September, she knew, so she must tell her father before long that she wanted to go back.

I guess it won't be hard to tell him, after all, she thought, feeling strangely unhappy. If he's forgotten my birthday, I don't believe he cares much about having me here with him, anyhow.

When she awoke on Wednesday morning, she could hardly believe that it was her birthday.

On my other birthdays I felt like a balloon floating around up in the air, she reflected sadly. Today I feel like a balloon that's had a pin stuck in it.

She got out of bed and went over to the mirror, and looked at herself solemnly. Eleven years old. That sounded much, much older than ten years old.

"Happy birthday, Pat," she said, aloud, making a little face at herself in the mirror.

While she and her father were eating breakfast, Mrs. Chandler called on the telephone. She said that she was going to Los Angeles to do some shopping and would like to have Pat go with her. Pat hesitated a moment before asking her father's permission to go. She wasn't sure that she wanted to go because she was sure that the aunts' presents would come by parcel post that morning. Still, the packages would keep until she got back, and it would be much better to spend a forgotten birthday in Los Angeles than alone all day with Robert.

Her father gave his consent to the trip readily, and gave her a five-dollar bill to put in her pocketbook in case, he said, she should see something for the house or something that she would like to have herself. Five dollars was a great deal more money than Pat had ever had before all at one time.

It's a birthday present after all, she thought. But it's no fun, because Father doesn't know that it's a birthday present.

It was quite a long drive to Los Angeles. As soon as they got to the city, Pat and Mrs. Chandler had lunch, and then they went to a shop in which Mrs. Chandler bought a dress after trying on about a dozen. Pat got very tired of waiting for her, because there was nothing interesting in the shop—only a lot of clothes for grownup people.

When Mrs. Chandler had finished buying the dress and a slip and some stockings, she took Pat to a fascinating shop in which Pat could happily have spent hours looking at things. However, she knew that Mrs. Chandler was in a hurry to start home in order to get back to the Base before dark, so Pat lingered only long enough to buy an ashtray shaped like an airplane for her father, a red necktie for Robert, and a bride and groom paper-doll book for herself.

It was really a disappointing trip.

All the way home Pat kept thinking how dreadful it would be if her aunts' packages hadn't come. When they finally got back to the Base and she had thanked Mrs. Chandler for taking her, she burst into the house.

"Robert," she called, "did any packages come for me?"

"Big box in Miss Pat's room," Robert answered from the kitchen. Pat sped down the hall. Darling Aunt Mary! Darling Aunt Sue!

She closed the door of her room behind her and stood gazing at the box with delighted eyes. She didn't even care what was in it—it was almost enough just to know that she had been remembered. The box, when finally opened, gave forth treasures that made her squeal softly with joy—a lovely doll in a pink silk dress with a long, full skirt; a stuffed panda that she loved on sight; white gloves from Cora; three new books and a lot of tiny packages that had been tucked in at the corners. Everything was beautifully wrapped and tied with elaborate bows.

When Pat finally heard her father come into the house, she started to call to him to come into her room to see all the things, and then decided not to.

It would make him feel terrible to find out now that it's my birthday, she thought.

Just in case he might come in, she hurriedly put the books under her bed where she could reach them after she had gone to bed, and pushed the panda under her pillow, because she was going to have it sleep with her. The other things she put carefully into the box in which they had been sent, and then shoved the box out of sight back against the wall of her closet.

She realized then that she would have to hurry to be ready in time for dinner, so she started her bath water running and dashed around getting out her fresh clothes while the tub was being filled. If she were having her birthday at home, she reflected, she would be wearing her best white dress with the peasant embroidery and her best white slippers.

I might as well dress up, she decided. Maybe wearing my best dress will make it seem a little bit more like a birthday.

When she had dressed and stood surveying herself in all her splendor in the mirror, tears were very near her eyes. I won't be able to eat any dinner, she thought miserably. A birthday dinner with no cake and candles!

"How very nice you look," her father said, smiling at her when she went slowly into the living room. "Did you have a nice time in Los Angeles?"

"Not very," Pat admitted. "We didn't have time to do anything much but buy Mrs. Chandler a dress. She bought another dark blue one, and she already has three dark blue ones. Why do older people always buy their clothes so much alike, I wonder? Aunt Sue always tries to find black dresses with little white dots in them, and Aunt Mary always buys black dresses with white lace collars. I can hardly tell their new clothes from their old ones."

Major Lowell laughed.

"That's a very pretty dress you have on," he told her. "By the way, won't you need some new clothes for school?"

Patricia's heart seemed to miss a beat. Tell him now, she ordered herself—and began hesitantly. "Father, I—"

Just then the doorbell rang, and Major Lowell said, getting up from his chair:

"That will be the Corricks. I meant to tell you this morning that I had asked them over for dinner to night, but you went off in such a hurry—"

Perhaps it's a surprise party, and there will be a cake with candles after all, Pat thought. She dashed to the door but the Corrick's didn't come in saying "Happy birthday," so she knew it wasn't a surprise party.

When the Corricks went out for the evening, they always took Spuds along, sound asleep. One of his parents would put him on a bed in the house in which they were visiting, and there he would sleep until someone picked him up to take him home. Usually he didn't even wake up then. Patricia couldn't get over that idea.

"Imagine going places and not even knowing it," she laughed, watching Mrs. Corrick plant pillows at strategic places on Pat's bed so that Spuds couldn't roll off.

The presence of the Corricks at the dinner table dispelled a little of Pat's homesickness.

I'm really having a party after all, she thought once or twice, in the laughter-filled dining room. It's just a shame that nobody knows it but me.

The dessert was ice cream, and Pat, seeing it, thought wistfully—more party. There was cake, too, but just slices, not a big, round cake with gay flickering candles to wish upon and blow out. There are probably lots of children in the world who never have birthday cakes, Pat thought sadly, but it's awful not to have one when you've been accustomed to them.

She closed her eyes for a second and thought of her cake the year before—it had had pink frosting and pink candles. She opened her eyes and reached hastily for her glass of water, because tears were just about ready to spill over. Pretending that she was having a birthday party really wasn't much good, she decided.

After the Corricks had gathered up Spuds and gone home, Major Lowell stopped Pat as she was about to tell him good night and start down the hall toward her room.

"Are you feeling all right tonight, Pat?"

"Oh, yes, of course," said Pat, in surprise, looking at him and thinking with a rush of love that he was so sweet and so good-looking and so dear that it

101

didn't really matter very much because he had forgotten her birthday.

"Well, I'm glad," he said. "I noticed you didn't eat much dinner and I was afraid you might be going to be sick on your birthday tomorrow."

Pat's eyes widened.

"On my what?" she gasped.

"Hey," Major Lowell said, laughing. "Don't tell me that little girls ever forget their birthdays."

"I—I hadn't forgotten," stammered Pat. "But tomorrow— Are you sure that TOMORROW is my birthday?"

"Well, I hope so," her father said, "for I'm taking tomorrow off on pass so that we can spend the whole day together doing just whatever you want to do."

"You—you hadn't said anything about it."

"No. I wasn't sure until late this afternoon that I could get a pass for the day, and I didn't want you to make plans until I was certain."

"But is TOMORROW—?"

Major Lowell smiled at her confusion and picked up the evening paper from the coffee table near his chair and read the dateline.

"It's tomorrow all right, sweetheart. This is Wednesday, August eleventh."

Then I must have figured wrong, Pat started to say and didn't, because it wasn't important now. The only important thing was the fact that her father hadn't forgotten her birthday, that he had remembered it, that he wanted to be with her all of the day.

"I'm so happy I'm about to burst!" she cried and sat down on his lap and kissed him eleven times— once for each year that would be indicated by her birthday TOMORROW.

Pat's birthday, the real one, was a lovely day.

"If I can really do just what I want today," Pat said radiantly to her father at the breakfast table, "I'd like to spend the whole day at the seashore."

"I thought that's what you'd say," her father chuckled. "We'll ask Robert to pack us a picnic lunch."

While Robert was getting the picnic basket ready, Major Lowell gave Pat what he called her "first" present, a record player and two albums of records.

"Robert will pick up your second present sometimes during the day," he told her. "It will be here when we come back from the beach."

"Goodness gracious," Pat said, her eyes bright with her delight in the record player, "this is enough present for two or three birthdays."

"You may not like the other one just at first," Major Lowell said, teasingly, and although Pat kept questioning him at intervals all during the long, glorious day on the beach, he wouldn't give her a single hint as to what the second present might be. All the way home, she wondered about it—what in the world could her father be giving her that perhaps she wouldn't like? Why would he give her something that he thought perhaps she wouldn't like?

She looked eagerly all around the house when they got back, and her father, correctly interpreting those anxious glances, said, laughing, "I suspect that Robert put him out in the patio."

"Him!"

Pat ran to the patio, of course, and both Major Lowell and Robert followed, to watch with amusement her first surprise when she saw "him." He tumbled out of a basket, straightened himself out with a shake and came waddling over to her to snuff at her sandals, a little black cocker spaniel, not much bigger than a minute, his tiny tail wagging furiously, his enormous eyes beseeching friendliness.

I don't like dogs. I don't want a dog, Pat thought, in dismay. She didn't want her father to be disappointed, so she stooped over and gingerly patted the shiny black head. The puppy was soft and silky. It snuggled against her hand and wiggled all over with delight at her caress.

"It's glad to see me—I think it's been lonesome," Pat said slowly. Suddenly she picked up the puppy, and let it cuddle down in her arms. Then she turned around to her father and Robert.

"I do like him," she said. "I like him better every minute. How long does it take a puppy to grow into a dog?

"Quite a long time," her father said, laughing, "and I think that you will like him even when he's full-grown."

"Well, maybe," Pat conceded doubtfully.

She couldn't bear to leave anything as small as that puppy alone, so she took him back to her room with her and let him play there while she was having her bath and getting dressed for dinner. It took her a long time to get dressed, because she had to stop every once in a while to laugh at the antics of the puppy and to separate him from all the things he wanted to chew.

"I'm going to name him Snuffy," she told her father at the dinner table, "because he snuffs at everything he sees."

The birthday evening was exciting, too. Robert had put flowers on the table and had baked a beautiful cake for the occasion, with white frosting and pink candles on it. Several people dropped in to bring birthday greetings and presents; the Corricks, General Chandler and Mrs. Chandler, Major Lowell's nice young aide, some of the hospital nurses.

"How in the world did everyone know it was my birthday?" Pat said to her father when at last they were alone. Then she laughed. "You don't have to tell me, I know. Everyone on an Air Force Base always knows everything about everyone else. Father, where is Snuffy going to sleep?"

"In the patio while the nights are warm. When they get cooler, we'll fix a place for him in the kitchen."

Together they put the puppy to bed in his basket, then hand in hand they went down the hall toward the bedrooms.

"It's been the most perfectly beautiful day," Pat said, squeezing her father's hand hard. "There's one thing that worries me, though—how can I ever get Snuffy ho—"

In dismay she broke off right in the middle of the word. She had been thinking about how to get Snuffy back to Middleport, but she hadn't meant to say so aloud. If only her father hadn't noticed, she thought.

He had noticed, of course.

He looked down at her for a long moment, and the light that had been in his eyes all evening faded.

"You mean you're worried about how to get Snuffy to Middleport when you go back?" he said slowly.

Pat nodded miserably.

"So you still want to go back, Pat?"

"I—I thought for school, you know. I—I was going to tell you in a few days, but I didn't mean to tell you tonight, on my birthday. Do you—will you mind too much?"

"No," Major Lowell said gently. "No, I shan't mind too much. If you are happier in Middleport than you are here, then that's where you should be."

105

"I'm not sure that I'm happier there—maybe it's just that I'm more used to it," Pat said.

Major Lowell laughed and stroked her hair back from her forehead.

"You needn't try to explain, dear," he told her. "You've been a good little sport about letting me transplant you—about giving it a try. Perhaps it's better for you to be with the aunts at any rate. Women know more about bringing up girls than men do. Don't worry about Snuffy—I'll figure out some way to get him to Middleport. Now I think you should run along to bed, sweetheart."

"I suppose so," sighed Pat, feeling simply awful. "I wish I could tell you how much I've loved my birthday."

"Your shining eyes told me. Good night, now."

"Good night," Pat said, but she didn't let go of her father's hand. She went on hesitantly: "It's a long way to go on a train all by myself."

She didn't know why she said that—she wouldn't be at all afraid to travel on a train by herself.

"Perhaps—if you could go with me—"

"I couldn't possibly get leave," Major Lowell said. "But I heard Major Joplin say the other day that his wife is going east sometime toward the last of this month. I'll find out when she is going and try to get reservations for you on the same train. I'll attend to it the first thing in the morning. Now good night again, and off to bed with you."

Pat threw her arms around him and, when he stooped down to her, kissed him hard. Then she flew down the hall to her own bedroom in a mighty effort to get there before the tears spilled over.

"I don't know why I'm crying," she sobbed to herself. "Ever since I left Middleport, I've wanted to go back, and now I am going back, so why am I crying? I guess it must be because I'm so relieved that I've finally told Father after all my worrying about it, and because he didn't seem to be too terribly sad and disappointed. Oh, dear, oh, dear, oh, dear!"

NEXT OF KIN

PAT WAS miserable all the following day. She felt so bad that she began to wonder whether perhaps she were coming down with a cold or a sore throat or something. Her nose wasn't stuffed up, though, and her throat didn't hurt when she swallowed. There was a big lump in it, to be sure, but it was the kind of lump she always had when she wanted to cry, not the kind for which she had to open her mouth for a doctor and say "ah-h-h."

All afternoon she found herself watching the clock to see whether it were not almost time for her father to come home. About five o'clock she went out to sit on the front step to wait for him. When he got out of the car and came up the walk, she thought suddenly, perhaps he couldn't get a reservation on the train for me.

She jumped up quickly and went to meet him.

"Everything's all taken care of," he said, smiling

down at her. "Mrs. Joplin is leaving on the twenty-seventh. I got a drawing room for you. You don't have to change trains—you'll go right through to Middleport on the same Pullman."

"I suppose I should write to Aunt Mary and Aunt Sue to tell them I'm coming," Pat said dully.

"We'll both write. Well, how's Snuffy been today?"

"Awfully cute," Pat answered.

All day she had been wanting to tell her father about the things Snuffy had done, but now the lump in her throat was so big that she didn't feel like talking. She didn't see how her father could be so cheerful as he was all evening. Didn't he realize, she wondered, that just two weeks from today she wouldn't be on the Base with him—that just two weeks from tonight she would be traveling farther and farther away from him, and that they might not see each other again for no-one-knew-how-long?

The tennis ball was bouncing around in her stomach again. She hadn't felt like that since she left Middleport.

She didn't feel very well the following morning, either. When she went over to the Corricks, she walked slowly instead of dashing along with her usual hop and skip.

Mrs. Corrick was washing windows, sitting on the top of a stepladder, her curly head tied up in a bright bandanna. Spuds was in his playpen, busy with his rubber blocks. When he saw Pat in the doorway, he shrieked with delight and began throwing his blocks in all directions.

"Come in," Mrs. Corrick said hospitably.

"I don't suppose I should. You're busy."

"I'd be glad to have an excuse to stop. Is it my

109

imagination, or are you a little pale under your suntan?"

"I feel sort of pale," Pat said and took a deep breath. "I'm going back to Middleport on the twenty-seventh of this month. That's in less than two weeks."

Mrs. Corrick's brown eyes widened.

"Well!" she said, after a moment. "How's it going to feel to be a civilian again after being in the Air Force all summer?"

"Sort of funny, I guess."

"When did you decide to go?"

"I've—I've always meant to go back before time for school to open. I just told Father two days ago."

"I don't suppose he was surprised," Mrs. Corrick remarked thoughtfully. "He's always thought you wouldn't stay."

"He has?" Pat asked in amazement. "He's never told me that. Why did he think I wouldn't want to stay?"

"I don't know exactly. Something about that he couldn't feel you loved him enough to stay because you always call him 'Father' instead of 'Daddy,' as you used to do when you were little."

"Oh," said Pat, and began picking up Spuds' blocks and putting them back into his playpen so that he could throw them out again. It was true that she never yet had said "Daddy." Once or twice, when she had first come to the Base, her father had asked her about it, half-teasingly, but when he had seen her embarrassment, he had not pressed her. Often, lately, the word had been on her lips, but she had held it back. She loved her father—she knew that—but the other word had been for the person she loved best in the world, and after all the years away from him she couldn't, couldn't say it.

She dodged a block that Spuds threw her way and looked at him lovingly. She would miss Spuds—

As the days went by with what seemed unusual rapidity, Pat realized that she would miss a lot of things about the Base—all her good friends, the exciting band, watching the great flag on the parade ground being lowered each evening at sundown. Elm Street in Middleport would seem pretty quiet after the continual excitement of Base Road. There would be no funny jeeps, no stuttering motorcycles, no friendly officers and nurses going by the big house on Elm Street. On Elm Street there would just be the milkman and the postman and an occasional grocery truck.

It will be nice, though, to live on a quiet street again, Pat told herself firmly.

She was to leave the Base on Friday morning. Early in the week Robert brought the big trunk into her room.

"I pack for you?" he asked. Robert had looked very solemn ever since he had been told that Pat was leaving.

"No, thank you, Robert. I think I can do it."

"You want help, you call."

"I will."

Still he lingered in the doorway, his forehead puckered in a puzzled frown.

"Miss Pat not like it here?"

"I love it here," Pat said, suddenly realizing that she did.

That's what's the matter with me, she thought, when Robert had gone. I like it here so much that I'm all mixed up. Of course I want to go back to Middleport —that's practically all I've been thinking about ever since I left there. I can hardly wait to see the aunts and Cora and all the girls and to start to school. It will probably seem strange just at first not to have D—— not to have Father coming in every evening calling, "Where's my girl?" the way he always does, but I'll get used to it after a few days, because I'll be so glad to be back.

She set her mouth in a firm, straight line and opened the trunk and began packing her books in the bottom drawer. When the shelf from which she had taken the books was empty, it looked so bare and lonesome that she couldn't stand it. She hurriedly put the books all back and decided she wouldn't pack until the next day. She ought to take Snuffy out for a walk anyhow, she told herself.

Snuffy was overjoyed to see her coming with his harness and leash. She walked him up to the general's corner, letting him stop to sniff at every bush along the way. As she was passing the Corrick house on the way back, Mrs. Corrick came out onto the porch and called to her to come in and have lunch.

"Snuffy's invited, too," she said.

Spuds was playing on a blanket on the floor. When Pat put Snuffy down beside him, the two babies sat staring at each other for a moment, then Spuds, with a delighted yelp, made a lunge for the puppy. Snuffy was so frightened that he scampered under the davenport. Spuds started after him on all fours, and when he found that he couldn't get under the davenport, too, he sat down on the floor and roared with disappointment and fury. Snuffy, meanwhile, from his shelter, howled with fright at the unfamiliar noise.

"We'd better get this stopped before the Military Police arrive," Mrs. Corrick said.

She picked up Spuds. Pat, by lying flat on her stomach, managed to pull Snuffy out from under the davenport. Mrs. Corrick sat down on the floor with Spuds on her lap and showed him how to pat the puppy's head. Spuds seemed to get the idea right away and patted and patted and patted. Snuffy wagged his tail and licked the baby's hand. All that was very nice until Spuds, who had learned how to pat so quickly, also learned to lick and, leaning forward, shot out his little pink tongue to Snuffy's nose.

"Just for that, young man," said Spuds' mother, "you shall go off for your nap five minutes earlier than usual, which is right now."

The two babies had really been very amusing together, but Pat hadn't laughed much at them. She wasn't hungry either, she found, after Mrs. Corrick had made sandwiches and Pat's favorite salad. She and Mrs. Corrick sat at the table for a long time, talking about everything but the fact that this was probably their last lunch together.

Later in the afternoon Mrs. Chandler called to ask Pat to go into Frankfort with her to go to a moving-picture show. After they had seen the film, Mrs. Chandler had to stop at a drugstore to purchase some things, so they got back to the Base rather late. As they were driving down Base Road, an ambulance passed them, siren screaming. It turned into the hospital drive.

"I hope there hasn't been a crash," Mrs. Chandler said, looking worried.

Pat wondered anxiously if there had been and whether any of the pilots she knew had been hurt. There hadn't been an accident since she had been on the Base. The thought that there probably had been one now made her feel dreadful.

After she had said good-by to Mrs. Chandler, she ran up the road to the house as fast as she could go.

Her father should be home—if anything had happened he would know all about it.

Her father hadn't come home yet.

"You late. He late," Robert said, when Pat dashed into the kitchen.

"Well, since Father's late, I'll still have time for my bath before dinner," Pat said. "Robert, was there a plane crash?"

"Paperboy just come by, tell me two ships bump each other in air—boom! Pilots hurt, maybe bad."

"Who were the pilots?"

"Not hear that. Air Force no tell until next of kin been notified."

"What's 'next of kin'?"

"Nearest relative. Wife, if any. Parents, guardian."

"Father hasn't any of those relatives," Pat said. She did a moment's sober thinking and then said, "I guess I'm Father's next of kin. Robert, if—if Father's plane, if—if Father—well, if Father were hurt, would I be notified?"

"Major too good pilot to bump other plane. You go take your bath and not think such things."

Of course Father's too good a pilot to bump into another ship, Pat thought, going down the hall toward her room, but another pilot might have bumped into him.

Feeling very much upset, she bathed and dressed, listening all the time for the sound of her father's car in the drive.

When she had finished dressing, she went to the living room and dialed the television set aimlessly. At half-past six, Robert entered the room.

"Everything ready now. Miss Pat better eat."

"I'm not very hungry yet, Robert."

"Well, Major be here any minute probably maybe. You wait some small time."

Robert went back to the kitchen, and Pat picked up a magazine and looked through it. She didn't seem to want to read any of the stories in it; she couldn't think about anything but the accident. Presently she put the magazine down on a table and went to stand by a window.

I simply can't imagine where Father can be, she thought. He's never been this late before. I suppose he worried like this about me the day everyone thought I'd disappeared. Oh, dear, I wish I hadn't forgotten to telephone that day—

The clock on the mantel struck seven times and, as it was striking, Robert reappeared.

"Dinner on table," he said firmly.

It seemed strange to Pat to be having dinner all alone. This is what Father will have to do all the time after I've gone, she thought. Probably he won't live here—probably he'll go to live in the Officers' Club, and some other family will have our house.

Pat didn't much like the idea of other people living in the house, of someone else having her very own room. She wondered what her father would do with the piano. He always said that it was hers, but it most certainly would cost a lot of money to have it shipped to Middleport. Besides, the aunts had a big grand piano, which they always said was Patricia's. Although the house was large, it certainly couldn't accommodate two pianos.

Where WAS her father?

"Has Father ever been this late before?" she asked Robert, when he brought in the dessert.

"No," Robert said gloomily.

115

Snow pudding was one of Pat's favorite desserts, but tonight she could only eat a spoonful.

She left the table, got Snuffy, and went to sit on the front steps. Snuffy wanted her to play with him, but she wasn't in the mood, so the puppy wandered down the lawn, found a stick and had a fight with it, growling at it and scolding it in the way that had never before failed to make Pat laugh. Tonight she didn't even watch him play—her eyes were fixed on the great hospital down Base Road.

As twilight deepened, lights etched the hospital windows in brightness. Snuffy tired of his game, curled up in Pat's lap and went to sleep.

Somewhere in that hospital are the pilots who were hurt today, Pat thought.

Where IS my father?

Why doesn't he come home?

The fear that had been in her heart ever since she had first heard about the crash grew until she felt it was choking her.

The outside world was almost completely dark now. Perhaps I'll feel better in the house with the lights on, she thought.

She gathered up Snuffy and went in.

"Maybe time for you to go to bed now," Robert suggested, coming into the living room.

"Oh, Robert, it isn't anywhere near my bedtime!"

"Well, maybe you telephone Captain Lattimer next door or Captain Corrick next door. They know where Major is maybe."

"I thought of that, but I'm sure they aren't home, because there aren't any lights in either of the houses."

"Maybe you telephone General."

"He flew to Seattle yesterday, and won't be home

until tomorrow. Mrs. Chandler was going back to Frankfort tonight to play bridge at the home of a friend. I would telephone her, but I don't know the friend's name—"

"Oh, well, Major come pretty soon now."

"I expect him to come any minute," Pat said staunchly.

Robert lingered, but neither he nor Pat could think of anything more to say, so presently he went out again. He's worried, Pat thought—he's as worried as I am.

The knowledge that Robert was worried made her own fear more acute. She pulled a chair over to one of the windows and sat on the edge of it, leaning forward to peer out into the darkness, her heart thumping painfully.

Surely, surely her father would come soon, unless perhaps—

Unless perhaps he would not come at all—not ever.

The breeze from the open window was warm, but suddenly Pat was cold and began to shiver. She picked up Snuffy and held his warm little body close, and listened in amazement to the sound of her own teeth chattering.

Then on the quiet evening air, there was another sound, footsteps coming up the walk, familiar steps, dearly familiar steps.

Pat jumped up, tumbling the outraged puppy from her lap. She ran the length of the room, out the door, and raced down the walk, her breath coming in little sobs.

"Daddy!" she cried, and then, as though she could never stop saying the word, "Oh, Daddy, Daddy, Daddy—"

Halfway up the walk her father stopped and caught her as she came flying toward him. He picked her up as he had done when she was a tiny girl. His voice, deep with tenderness, made Pat cry harder than ever.

"Why, Pat! What's the matter with my girl? Don't cry so hard, sweetheart. Tell me what has happened."

"Nothing's happened," sobbed Pat, winding her arms tightly around his neck. "I'm just crying because you've come home and because I love you so much—"

"Then I could do with a bit less strangling," Major Lowell laughed.

He sat down on the step and put Pat on his knee as he wiped the tears off her face with his handkerchief. Then she told him how frightened she had been.

"I ought to be shot," he said, when she had finished. "The truth of the matter is, I had lost all track of time. I had no idea how late it was. You see, two of my boys were in that crash this afternoon. I came in from the field in the ambulance with them and stayed with them in the hospital until the doctors were sure that they were going to live. I should have let you know. I'm deeply ashamed."

"It's all right now," Pat said happily, with her head against his shoulder. Then she added shyly, "Did you —did you hear what I said when I ran down the walk?"

"Yes," said Major Lowell, his arms tightening around her, "I heard it and I liked it very, very much."

"It's funny," Pat said wonderingly. "All the time I was saying it and running to meet you, something was happening inside of me. I didn't know what it was then, but I've been thinking about it and now I do know. It was that I began not to want to go back to Middleport. It was that I began to want to stay here."

"Now, look," Major Lowell began, "I suppose you've been thinking that Middleport will seem pretty quiet to you after a summer on the Base, and you're right. It will seem quiet for a while, but just for a little while. After a few days, you'll almost forget that you were ever away."

"That isn't what I was thinking at all," Pat said, raising her head from his shoulder to shake it decisively.

"Besides, you know," her father continued, "I have no idea how long I'll be stationed on this Base. I think I'll be here for quite a while, but I don't know that I will be. I might possibly be sent somewhere else tomorrow, sent to some place that you wouldn't like at all."

"It isn't the Base," Pat said patiently. "It's that I want to live with you and be a family."

"But you love Aunt Mary and Aunt Sue so much, and should love them—"

"Of course I love them. I love everyone in Middleport. But the aunts could come to California to spend the winter—I think they would like to do that. They don't like cold weather and snow—they're always afraid of falling on the ice and breaking their bones. If I wanted to, I could go back to visit sometimes—"

"You've always called Middleport home, Pat."

"I know," Pat nodded. "I found out tonight, though, while I was waiting for you, that it doesn't seem like home any more. No place would seem like home any more unless you were there, because you're my next of kin, and I love you best in all the world. Please, please, please, will you let me stay?"

119

"What do you think?" her father asked, holding her close.

"I think you'll let me," Pat said, and added contentedly, "My goodness, the way things have turned out, I'm certainly glad I didn't do all my packing this afternoon—"